ANGEL SONG

SARA SHANNING

Sara Shanning

Imagenation
is freedom ♡

 Created with Vellum

ACKNOWLEDGMENTS

I suppose we all dream of fairy tales Once Upon A Time.
This book is dedicated to my daughter, Reese. She asked for
a little romance and this book was the result.
I tried to write a normal romance.
Alas, it was not meant to be.

CHAPTER 1

She had not fallen, but she had lost her way. Forgotten the path that would take her back to everything she knew. Nor could she remember the things she knew that she should.

It was an odd place to be in, wandering with no direction, knowing you should have one.

A melody without words played in her head as the cold of the earth began to touch her, a whisper over her skin that caused a curious tremble to flow through her body. A twinge began in her stomach she realized might be hunger. There were scents making the air seem alive in a way she was unfamiliar with.

Breeon walked over the tangled web of the forest floor and through the towering rise of pines, something deep within her telling her that things were changing quickly, and it would not be much longer before she could no longer continue as she was.

If she could only remember what she had been doing...

A flutter surfaced in her mind, then was quickly drawn back before she could quite grasp what the meaning of it was.

The longer she walked, the more the light that hovered around her dimmed, the deeper the shadows became in her mind, and the hazier her memory became until finally, there was nothing more than the forest and the cold, and a heavy silence that frightened her. The melody too had quieted so that it was only a faint hum in the far recesses of her mind.

Shaking, clutching at her bare arms, Breeon stepped free of the trees and stared ahead at a log cabin with smoke drifting from the chimney. She watched the sky welcome the smoke, understanding dawning that smoke meant fire and fire meant warmth.

Pinecones pricked at the bottoms of her feet, snow mashed and left icy wetness clinging to her skin. If she had looked, she would have seen that the hem of her dress was torn and wet.

The numbness was still there in her mind, shielding her from most of the pain. Still, the pain was enough to propel her forward to the cabin, up the steps and to the door.

Here, she paused. Anyone watching would have noticed the last of the light around her fade, seen the shiny flecks of gold glimmering in her hair and on her skin wink out, and the majestic sheen of her already out-of-place dress become nothing more than a beautiful, tattered gown worn by a woman who had obviously lost her mind, wandering around in the woods without the proper attire.

For Breeon, it was the end of who she had been and the beginning of who she was now.

If one had asked, she would have been unable to answer whether she had knocked or not, or if the man who opened the door to her somehow had sensed that she stood there, waiting for the light and warmth inside to breathe over her with the sweeping motion of the door.

His eyes were startled, his gaze curious and a bit alarmed as they took in her long fall of golden hair and the cascading skirt of her dress, her only shield against the last days of the winter that enveloped everything beyond the stretch of his porch.

Looking beyond her, he tried to determine where she could have come from. There was no horse. Footprints were clearly visible in the clinging snow leading back into the dense forest beyond.

He could not, of course, leave her standing there, and so he curled his hand around the cold skin of her upper arm and guided her inside to stand before the fire, leaving her to retrieve a blanket from the back of the settee to drape over her shoulders.

The seam of the dress that ran across the middle of her back was low enough to reveal strange bruising and cuts near her shoulder blades that looked partially healed.

The bareness of her feet had also not gone unnoticed over the short walk. There was no one to call for help and none of her injuries seemed to require immediate attention. The solitude was why he had sought his cabin and there would be no one to turn to.

So instead, he brewed hot water, watching as she sank down before the shifting shimmer of the fire and huddled into the blanket. Where she could possibly have come from was a mystery. There were no other homes for miles, no matter the direction one took. Therefore, he concluded that somehow whatever unit she had been with had perhaps come across trouble and he would question her when color was back in her cheeks.

He brought her tea, kneeling between her and the flames. Her eyes when she lifted them were the same color as the lighter topaz of the fire and he was unsure at first if it was the reflection of that, or if her eyes were flecked with gold. "The tea will warm you," he urged as he held it out.

She was hesitant in taking it, her hand emerging from the blanket slowly to touch the side of the mug as though she were unsure of what it was.

The heat against her fingers was like bringing the fire closer to her and Breeon brought the mug closer, curling her hand around it, peering down into the liquid.

She had seen people drink, and it was those images trapped far back in places she could no longer remember that told her what to do. There was honey in the vapor that rose from the mug. It was pleasant and she held the cup still for awhile to inhale. Something familiar whispered as gently as the steam from the tea, and with a soft sigh, she sipped at the liquid.

Like the blanket around her shoulders and the flames before her, it soothed the cold of the winter that had wrapped around her and made her weary.

She was hardly aware of the man near her as she sipped the comforting liquid. He was busy moving the settee closer to the fire and spreading another blanket over the cushions.

She seemed half asleep to him when he took the almost empty mug from her, and she did not argue when he suggested that she lie down to sleep. Not knowing what to do about the heavy wetness of her hem, he watched her as she curled into the blanket and settled her cheek on a pillow.

He could not recall when he had ever seen a woman so beautiful. There were questions to be answered, of course, but she did not seem to be hurt and there was little he could do at such a late hour.

He added more wood to the fire and left her for his own bed. Tomorrow he would worry about the woman's appearance and what he would have to do about it.

Her arrival was placing him in a precarious position. Few knew of his whereabouts, but always he had to think about his reputation. Morally, he would turn away no one in need, male or female, but the lack of a chaperone put him at a disadvantage.

If anyone else was present, there would be no need for concern. Without one, even the arrival of one of his men would mean consequences neither he nor the mysterious woman were prepared for, no matter what the explanation for how she had come to be in his cabin.

He had been gone mere days. It seemed that now he would have to make the choice to leave, to discover where she had come from and return her there, and then return to his own home and forget that she had ever knocked on his door at all.

CHAPTER 2

*E*nlin tossed the pieces of split wood in his hands toward the pile on the ground, frowning at the two horses on the path coming from the forest, bearing his men. This was exactly what he had been afraid of.

Rylan alone would have made things easier, but Telphee was adamant about duty and would have zero regard for the circumstances.

Bending to gather wood, Enlin filled his arms and climbed the stairs to the door. The woman had been sleeping when he had checked on her. The sound of the axe may have awakened her, but if not, he hoped to have time to warn her of what was coming next.

She was awake, her topaz eyes cloudy with sleep and confusion. Her cheeks were no longer as pale as silk sheets but were rosy. Her long hair was messy, but not in an unappealing way.

If things had been different, Enlin might have felt himself drawn to her if they had met under normal circumstances. As things were, he had defied convention for many years already.

Outside the door, boots thudded against wood and one of the horses snuffled.

"I should warn you..." Enlin began, but her head had turned at the sound of the horse and a look of delight had come over her. She tossed the blanket aside to rise and was at the door and opening it before Enlin realized her intent.

The look of surprise on Rylan's face was comical, but Enlin could find no mirth to chuckle, for beside Rylan, Telphee's face had morphed from a fierce frown, to confusion, to triumph.

Without a single word, Enlin knew that a victory would not be his. Telphee would have his way. Still, he steeled himself for a fight and moved to stand behind the woman.

"Sir?" Rylan, of course, would give him the grace to offer an explanation.

Telphee lifted a hand, shaking his head with narrowed eyes.

"Her appearance is enough on its own to condemn you. You needn't bother with an explanation."

Enlin addressed Rylan. "She came to the door last night, dressed as she is. No shoes, no covering. I haven't any idea where she has come from. She was still sleeping... on the settee... when I left the cabin this morning."

"It matters not," Telphee stated firmly. "Lady, please sit. We have much to discuss." Telphee indicated that the woman should proceed them, but she did not move.

"Are you well?" Rylan asked, leaning forward slightly to peer more closely at the woman. Enlin moved closer to her side, placing a hand around her arm to steady her, fearing she would faint.

"I do not seem to remember," she said softly. Her voice was melodic and entrancing. Enlin stared at her as she spoke, wishing that she would continue.

The impatience was obvious when Telphee spoke, "What is it that you do not remember? That you are not well? You realize that makes absolutely no sense at all." He waved a hand at Enlin. "Take her to a seat."

She lifted her eyes to his and Enlin wondered if he had ever looked into eyes so clear or innocent. If his mind had not been quite so focused on the scenario playing out, he may have seen that beyond the color of her irises a light still shone that would have further set her apart from any others that he had looked into.

Instead, resigned, Enlin asked her gently if she would sit and she complied, with one more glance toward the door as Rylan shut it before following them to sit as well.

"Sir, you must know what I am going to say." Telphee had always relished his position of upholder, the vast bank of knowledge about the rules and propriety of the Kingdom his one gift. There was no one else that rivaled his expansive expertise and so he had long maintained his position.

Enlin tried to think of something that would be sufficient to persuade Telphee away from his course.

Telphee addressed the woman. "Lady, do you understand who this man is?"

"Should I remember him?" she asked curiously.

A look was exchanged between Rylan and Telphee. Rylan lifted a hand to stop Telphee from speaking. His rank was higher, although he did not often use it to gain the advantage. "Lady, could you please explain to us where you have hailed from?"

"I am sorry, but I do not remember."

"You came from the woods," Enlin pressed. "Surely you were with a group? Did you get separated? Were you over-taken by someone who meant harm?"

From outside of the cabin, one of the horses made noise again.

Her eyes dashed to the door and her hand lifted to touch her mouth. "I do believe I would like to speak to the horses." A small smile spread beneath her fingers.

"Don't be ridiculous, Lady," Telphee scoffed. "One does not speak to horses."

The smile faded and her hand fell back to settle in her lap.

She looked at Telphee, her eyes blinking, her mouth slightly parted. She contemplated his words, one small part of her mind rejecting the possibility as untrue, but if he was saying it was true, why would he lie?

She had listened to the soft nickers of the horses, feeling a flutter of joy wing to life inside of her each time. She longed to run her hand over one, to feel the power and the gentle spirit. Was that also not the truth? Perhaps she knew nothing at all about horses.

Breeon felt cold suddenly and wished she were closer to the fire or had the softness of the blanket still around her.

She did not understand the presence of the two new arrivals before her. They seemed quite serious, but she understood only that she understood nothing at all.

"Let us skip the pleasantries, shall we?" Telphee stood, clasping his hands at his back, and looking down his nose at the woman. "You and the Prince have been alone in this cabin, without a chaperone. Of course, this puts both of your reputations in a compromised position. There is only one solution."

Enlin closed his eyes and took a deep breath. He could not in good conscience allow the woman to be ruined when nothing at all had happened. Nor could he speak in front of Telphee and Rylan the truth about why he had to find another way than what he knew Telphee had already determined would happen.

"I believe I knew a Prince once..."

Opening his eyes, Enlin looked at her in surprise. He knew all the neighboring Kingdom's Princes and surrounding aristocracy. If she was of noble birth, he would have come across her at some time in his life.

There had been peace among the Kingdoms for decades

and so it was common to celebrate together. In past years there had been far more intent behind the festivities as the King had become more persistent in his pursuit of a bride for his son.

Enlin knew he would not have forgotten her if he had met her before. Which meant she was not of noble birth. He snapped his gaze to Telphee. Would this matter? It would leave her in ruin but would save both from a destiny he had done everything he could to avoid.

Telphee gave him a tight smile, his next words showing that he had guessed the direction of Enlin's thoughts. "Her dress and manner speak of noble birth, Sir. Your hopes have no foundation." He stood and addressed Rylan. "Let us prepare for the journey back. I will care for the horses. You see to the Prince and the Lady."

Enlin rose and went to the kitchen. He put on the kettle and then began to put together some bread, cheese, and several thick slices of ham. It was too early for such fare, but he guessed that she may not have eaten for awhile, and they had a long journey ahead.

Rylan had followed him. "Do you know who she is, Sir?" he asked in a low voice.

Enlin shook his head. "Telphee moves too quickly. We must inquire of the neighboring Kingdoms. Somewhere, she has a home, and her family must be worried about her."

"He will allow you no other choice, Sir." Rylan poured the tea and followed Enlin with mugs back to the hearth.

Enlin set the tray down and sat across from the woman. "Could you tell us your name?"

He watched her contemplate his question, her brows drawing in for a few moments before her eyes brightened and she smiled.

"Yes! It is Breeon."

Enlin glanced at Rylan, who gave a small shake of his head. It was not a common name, nor was it one that he had heard before in any of the surrounding Kingdoms. Could she have come from farther away? And how would she have ended up wandering alone in the woods with no escort or procession?

"I am Rylan, aide and royal guard to the Prince." He indicated the man at his side. "This is, of course, Prince Enlin. Telphee is the man outside caring for the horses. Could you tell us where you hail from, Lady Breeon?" Rylan handed her a mug of the tea.

Again, the confusion clouded over her face. This time, no light lit her eyes, no smile came to her lips. She shook her head. "I cannot."

"You must have family that is looking for you," Rylan suggested, pushing the tray a bit closer to her.

Breeon looked at the contents on the tray in front of her, her mind supplying the names of the offerings even though she had never tasted any of them. She understood that she was to eat and reached for a piece of the thickly sliced cheese.

It was strange to touch, soft but firm, and the scent and taste were sharp. She liked it immensely. The tea was warm and as comforting as she had found the fire and the blanket to be.

Content, she finished the small piece she had taken and smiled at both men watching her. "It is very good." She had forgotten the question that they had asked.

"Lady Breeon, please tell me that you are comprehending what will soon happen in your future?" Rylan asked, his face serious.

Breeon liked this man much better than the one who had gone out to care for the horses. His manner was kind, his dark eyes were gentle but not weak. There was a strength in him that told her that he could be trusted. It was clear that he respected the Prince by his side.

The Prince exuded a different kind of strength. It held

more power and more confidence. Really, she had no idea why the two seemed so somber, nor had she any inkling at all as to what they were talking about.

Her future was as blank as her past seemed to be. She had not forgotten so much that she didn't know one's future could not be seen.

That the man was a Prince made him no different than any other. It gave him a position of power, but position meant nothing about a person's heart.

Neither of the men had touched anything on the tray and thinking that they were waiting on her to finish what she wanted, Breeon took another piece of the cheese.

"Forgive me for not having the answers that you seek. I can only recall my name..."

The Prince abruptly stood up. "They'll require me to marry you," he stated, holding her gaze steadily. She noticed for the first time that his eyes were as dark and rich as the green of the pine trees in the forest.

One dark eyebrow lifted above a green iris. "Did you hear what I said, Lady Breeon?" Enlin hoped by using her name, he would capture her full attention. She had not so much as blinked at his announcement. He had a fleeting thought that he should be disturbed that she had not. Perhaps her arrival had been intended to produce the outcome Telphee would demand.

Looking into her clear eyes made him feel a fool for thinking such.

"Your eyes remind me of the forest," she said. She gave a smile to Rylan. "Your Prince is like the trees of the forest, is he not?"

"I'm sorry, Lady, I do not understand?"

She leaned forward to answer Rylans question, a shimmer flashing through her eyes. "The trees that stand for centuries. Tall and powerful. With roots that are deep and branches that spread to offer cover, protection, and life to everything around them. And you stand beside him."

The topaz of her eyes darkened, the flecks melding with each other in a mesmerizing play of gold that Enlin could not look away from. "An army stands around you, Prince. It is strong and expansive. Your Kingdom is a haven for all who seek it." She blinked several times, the topaz fading back to clear sunshine. "Oh." Confusion flickered over her face again. "I am supposed to be here, aren't I? For just a moment I remembered, but now I cannot recall what I held in my mind..." Her words trailed away, the tea and cheese in her hands forgotten.

Enlin was glad that it was Rylan at his side and not Telphee. She spoke in riddles, and none of them comforting. Her words could mean that a plot was playing out with either of them as the pawn after all. He had no idea how one would go about making her a part of one without her knowledge. Or, if she was playing the game, manipulating him with confusion.

He paced away toward the fire, using the poker to shift the blackened wood. If they were leaving, he had things that had to be prepared. Clothes for her would be a problem. He had nothing suitable. They couldn't very well take her without shoes upon her feet or a cloak to shield her from the winter cold.

"Please eat," he urged, turning back. "Rylan and I must prepare for the journey."

There wouldn't be much. He had traveled to the cabin alone, leaving a message for Rylan and leading his horse away before dawn and the morning stirrings of the Kingdom.

With Rylan in his suite, he spoke freely. "Her words trouble me. She seems to remember nothing, and then speaks things that make no sense."

Rylan nodded. "Yes. We must be wary despite her

seeming innocence. She is quite captivating though, is she not Your Highness?"

Enlin frowned as he searched through his belongings for an extra cloak. He would not give Rylan the satisfaction of a response. They would have the time of the journey to attempt to gain further answers. Once they reached the castle, he would have little time to find a way to delay the inevitable.

Unbeknownst to Rylan or Telphee, the marriage being thrust into his future could not be allowed to happen. The consequence of the nuptials should he be unable to stop them troubled him. This part of his life, of his future, had been decided for him years ago on one of many undiscovered expeditions into the night that he had made in his youth.

One night long ago he had left the castle a boy seeking an adventure, on the verge of manhood. He had returned as a man with a secret to guard for the protection of his Kingdom.

CHAPTER 3

"She'll have to ride with you, Sir."

The horses were packed, and Rylan had bound Breeon's feet and had found an extra cloak for her. She had seemed unconcerned with the conversations that had flowed around her as the final preparations had been made.

The castle was not far, only a couple of hours on horseback, but Telphee was impatient. Enlin could well imagine the preparations already finalized in Telphee's head and the speech of triumph that would be presented to the King.

He was attempting to come up with a speech of his own, but none had felt sufficient.

Enlin watched Breeon greet his horse, stroking the muzzle as though they had been friends for years. His horse nuzzled against her. He could see her mouth moving, a murmur of words he could not make out soothing his normally spirited horse and making him as calm as a docile mare.

Rylan helped Breeon mount and Enlin swung up behind her, struggling to maintain distance between their bodies. That proved to be impossible. Nor did she seem particularly worried about their proximity. She snuggled back against him and pulled the cloak closer around her, sighing as though it was the most natural thing to do in the world.

It was not natural for him at all. Enlin had made it a point to keep women at arms length since he had learned that there would never be one in his future. He was uncomfortable with such closeness.

Her hair was soft against his jaw. She smelled fresh, though he wasn't quite sure what that encompassed. And while she was relaxed, he was not. He spent the entire journey holding his body tense and upright, trying to keep his arms from closing her in as though he had a right to hold her.

Never mind that if Telphee had his way he would. He could not marry her. And still, he could think of no solution that would solve anything.

The castle came too soon, and not soon enough. Telphee refused to take any route but the front gate to enter, stating that servant's entrances were beneath them and the Prince should be mindful of such things.

Breeon thought the castle was beautiful and said so. The stone walls were draped with intricately embroidered flags depicting fierce lions, and ivy had made a home in long stretches over the walls.

The guards greeted their Prince with bows of respect, welcoming him home. She could hear warmth in their voices. There were smiles upon the faces of the people they passed. The children waved.

"They love you," Breeon said, twisting to see Enlin's face. "They are my people." There was mutual affection in his voice. Breeon turned back to take in everything before her. Inside of her something familiar had sparked, but though she tried she could not decipher the meaning. There was something about the majestic rise of the castle ahead, the clean gathering of stalls along the path, and the clusters of the people that made it all welcoming, and somehow familiar in a way.

All that she could see was well cared for. Fires burned to ward off the cold for those working. There were stone gardens and fountains scattered about, and even though much of the vegetation, dormant for the winter season had been cut down, care had been taken to make each one visually appealing.

The castle itself rose high above them and spread its arms out into the Kingdom grounds. There were carvings and scrollwork in the stone, the windows were wide and high, and colorful glass gave the appearance of jeweled lions.

Stablehands rushed forward as they drew up to take the horses. Rylan dismounted and helped Breeon from her horse. Large wooden doors decorated with wrought iron had been opened and several of what she thought were castle staff had come out to greet them.

Breeon smiled at them all. She could see curiosity in their eyes as they looked back at her, but none meant any disrespect.

"Your Highness," they greeted Enlin, dropping into bows and curtsies.

Telphee stepped forward. "Take the Lady to a room and make her presentable for the King immediately," he ordered.

Nods were given and hands grasped gently at her arms to lead her into the castle. Breeon looked over her shoulder at Enlin, hearing words that had not penetrated until that moment. 'They'll require me to marry you.'

"Oh..," she breathed. That could not be. It was not allowed.

Startled, she looked at one of the girls at her side. She did not know her. Breeon realized then that she did not know anyone, but somehow, she did know that she could not marry.

There was little that she could do. She cast about in her mind for how to proceed but could think of nothing.

Breeon was taken to a room with soft yellow and green tapestries on the walls. Long curtains in the same colors fell around the large bed and wrapped artfully around each of the four posts.

A divan was cushioned in the yellow, as was the seat set before a wide vanity next to an expansive window. The window was draped with heavy embroidered curtains that fell to pool on the floor. Rich rugs divided sections in the large room.

It was a pleasant merging of colors and richness, and Breeon felt welcomed by the decor.

"My lady." One of the girls curtsied as she beckoned to the seat of the vanity. "A bath is being drawn. May I untangle your hair?"

A mirror curved in arches over her head. Breeon stared at the woman looking back at her in the glass. The face was unfamiliar, but the blinking of the eyes told her that it was her.

Behind her, the servant waited with clasped hands for her to respond.

On the vanity, a gilded brush and comb waited. Clear bottles held liquid, a handheld mirror lay facedown beside the brush, glittering with a flower made of gems. Jeweled clips and combs graced a glass tray.

"I do not belong here," Breeon said, looking up at the reflection of the girl.

"My lady, if I may, if the Prince has brought you here, then you do belong here."

'They'll require me to marry you.' She heard the words again in her mind. The wording signified that he did not have a choice. Breeon pressed her eyes closed, pulling at the memories that she had. At other things that he had said.

Not him. The one called Telphee. He had commented on her appearance.

"I don't understand," Breeon whispered. She opened her eyes and turned to face the girl. "What is wrong with my appearance?" she questioned.

The girl shook her head. "My lady?"

Realizing that she still wore the cloak, Breeon un-clasped it and slid it from her shoulders. "Why is it that my appearance dictates that the Prince must marry me?"

The servant's eyes widened. Her eyes darted away, first to the left and then to the right. They were blue, as dark as the blueberries that grew in the forest in the spring.

"Please, tell me," Breeon asked again.

Color tinged the girl's cheeks. There was a shyness in her eyes when she finally looked back at Breeon. "My lady, I am only a servant."

"I need to understand," Breeon pleaded. "I do not remember anything more than knocking on a cabin door. I did not know who was inside. Your Prince simply gave me tea and a blanket and that was all. The man Telphee came in the morning with Rylan and now I am here, and the Prince says that they will require him to marry me. Why?"

The girl's face was red now. She was grasping at her skirts. "My lady, you should not speak of such things to a servant. It isn't done!"

Breeon reached out to take one of the girl's hands, squeezing it. "If you will not tell me, who will? I am no greater than you."

The girl blinked furiously. She swung her head to look over her shoulder, then leaned forward and whispered, "My lady, you are no servant. Your dress is fine and made of fabric unlike anything I have ever seen. You are of noble blood."

"Those things tell me nothing. Please answer my question."

The servants voice dropped lower so that Breeon had to strain to hear. "One cannot stay alone as a woman with a Prince overnight without consequence, my lady." The words were whispered in a rush and the title was bit off with a frustrated breath and the girl curtsied again, more than once.

"Why ever not if one is only cared for and sleeps?"

"My lady," the girl hissed. "Please! It is just not done! Not by one with your stature and position!"

More confused than ever, Breeon opened her mouth to further inquire as to the meaning of the girl's words when a door to the side of the room opened and a second girl appeared.

"My lady, your bath is ready."

"Do not ask any more questions, my lady. Your secrets are not safe with everyone." The girl at her side whispered the words hurriedly as she accompanied Breeon into the next room.

The words gave her pause and Breeon tried to make sense of everything that she could recall as she sank down into the heated water. She watched the two young women as they darted around, preparing clothing for her and bringing accessories to place against the gown, one after another before they finally decided which they liked.

Breeon noticed watching the two girls that the one who had explained things to her seemed to be of a lower rank. The one who had drawn her bath ordered the younger about and did not have the same shy openness about her. Breeon concluded that she could not trust the older.

She was glad when the shy servant was the one to gently wash her hair and help her to finish bathing.

Finally, she was dressed, and Breeon was glad that she had had help with the layers of clothing that she did not understand. Her hair was combed and gathered at the sides with clips. One of the bottles was sprayed at her neck and wrists. Shoes were placed upon her feet.

Breeon wondered where all of it had come from.

"I will go ahead and let them know that she is ready," said the one that Breeon had determined that she could not trust.

Alone for a moment, Breeon asked the question that had hovered on her tongue. "What secret must I keep?"

The girl tossed a look around the hallway, hushing Breeon. "What you told me about being alone with the Prince. You must tell no one. Your secret is safe with me, my lady. The Prince is well loved, but there are always enemies."

CHAPTER 4

*B*reeon found the castle layout to be confusing. There were halls and stairwells, and then more halls and stairwells, before they finally stopped in front of a closed door with a stern man waiting with a disapproving look that he cast over both. She had asked the servant's name and been told it was Velynn.

Her further questions had been hushed and Velynn had told her that it was not proper for a Lady to converse with her servants, and that if she must talk, she should do so within the privacy of her chambers when they were alone.

"The King has been waiting," the man scolded coldly.

The servant curtsied and said not a word as she left Breeon's side.

"You will address the King as 'Your Majesty,' you shall speak only when spoken to, and at no time may you find anything he says unfavorable. Do you understand?"

Breeon stared into the cold eyes of the man before her. "Who are you?" she asked.

"I am the King's Steward." It was said haughtily. Breeon decided she liked him less than she liked Telphee.

The room they entered had a fire burning in a wide stone

fireplace. Several large stuffed chairs faced it. One held a man with similar features to the younger man leaning against the mantle that arched over the fire. Enlin. He looked very serious.

The Steward placed himself between her and the King, who had stood.

"Leave us, please," Enlin ordered.

The man beside her tensed. His nod and jaw were stiff, his back straight and taut as he left the room and pulled the heavy door closed behind him, leaving her alone with Enlin and the King.

Breeon faced the King squarely, taking him in. He was tall and had obviously passed on his dark hair and eyes to his son, although his hair was lined with gray. His apparel was casual, as though he had been outside. It was not what she expected for a King, although she wasn't sure where that thought originated from. She didn't know any Kings after all, did she?

No crown graced his head, no royal emblem was attached to his clothing. Breeon noticed that his eyes, though as green as his sons, were shadowed, and she stepped back when she felt as though the shadows left his eyes to flow into hers.

A heaviness filled her and the space around her wavered. Breeon did not realize that her knees had given out until strong arms wrapped around her, keeping her from falling.

"Are you quite all right?" Enlin asked, his breath warm on her cheek, his eyes concerned.

She was not, because the shadows had curled into her and whispered their secrets. "Your Kingdom is falling," Breeon whispered, feeling the distress of the truth as deeply as the memories she had lost.

"What is this that you speak of?" the King demanded, moving forward with long, sure strides to stand before her.

Holding onto Enlin for support, Breeon tried to gather

the swirls in her head to make sense of them. "Forgive me, Your Majesty, but I do not have the answers you seek."

She had not done as the Steward had directed. She had spoken first and said something unfavorable. Why could she not remember who she was? How was it that she had just felt the fate of a Kingdom that she knew nothing about? Things such as this were impossible.

"You must explain yourself, Lady Breeon," Enlin said fervently.

"My son is right. Considering the position that you have found yourself in, I must know that you are not here as an act of treason." The fierceness on the King's face reminded her of the lions that roared from their flags and tapestries.

Enlin guided her to a chair and Breeon gladly sat. The fire burned into the air inside of its stone walls. She could feel the heat, but it did not warm her as the one had in the cabin.

"I can hardly explain things to myself," she began. "I can feel that there is something there if I could only just take hold of it long enough to comprehend the meaning." Closing her eyes, she tried again to draw out buried memories and bring them to the surface.

Sighing in frustration, she shook her head and opened her eyes to meet the Kings. "In your son I saw a great army, like the trees of the forest. Powerful and vast. In your eyes, I saw darkness and stone crumbling, but the darkness is not my own to explain. It is yours."

The flames of the fire burned in the Kings eyes. He scowled at her as she gave her speech, but Breeon felt no fear. "I have no idea what we are to do with you," he stated when she spoke no more.

Enlin had crossed his arms and stood straight and tall, his face unreadable. "You must realize that you are not helping yourself."

"I am not here to bring anyone harm." She knew that. It

did not matter what else she did not know. Neither of the men before her meant her any harm. Enlin had welcomed her when apparently, he should not have. His father had welcomed her into his castle and offered the same hospitality.

The King began to pace. "Telphee will have already spun his tale. It cannot be undone. The whispers will have already reached the peasants." He stopped abruptly, pivoting to face Breeon. "I must make it clear that if we do find that you are guilty of treason, you will be imprisoned."

There was passion in the King's movements. Her words had wrought fear to rise. "What things are at play, Your Majesty, that distress you so?"

"Have you no respect for formality, Lady Breeon? I am a King. You cannot ask such questions. You are quite unlike any of the nobility I have ever encountered."

"Oh," Breeon breathed out. "Forgive me, Your Majesty. I am afraid that I seem to know nothing of decorum in such circumstances." She felt suddenly very tired and sank back further into the chair, pulling her legs up to tuck them beneath her, glad that the many layers while bulky, were not a hindrance to movement. There had been no layers beneath the dress the servants had taken from her.

"Nothing is familiar to me, though at times I have felt that they are. I have only questions and I hear the riddles that I speak. Perhaps the forgetting is easier than the attempt to recall anything at all."

The King gave a shake of his head, murkiness lurking deep in his eyes. "No, forgetting is not easy at all. Tell me which Kingdom you have come from? It must be one of those far from the boundaries of our lands."

"I do not remember, Your Majesty."

Enlin was watching her closely, and she wondered if he thought her guilty of treason. There was a heaviness in his eyes as well, but it was different than that of his fathers.

Breeon tried to gather the pieces of what she knew and see them clearly, but she could not.

"We will question you again on the morrow. I can see that you are tired," the King said and moved to open the door. "Call for her attendants and place guards at her door tonight," he ordered whoever waited beyond.

Breeon was glad to be taken back to the solitude of the room and she allowed the servants to help her to dress for bed, burrowing beneath the luxurious coverlets to sleep, grateful as the questions faded away.

CHAPTER 5

"*Y*ou should have held your tongue, Telphee. Now, this cannot be undone, and we may have a traitor about to become a member of the royal family."

"Then she will be imprisoned for treason, Your Majesty. And if she is not a part of some plot, then you will have exactly what you have been asking your son to find for years; a bride."

"I cannot marry her!" Enlin interjected. He had been standing by silently while Telphee and his father had their argument. He had thought of no good way to convince his father that he must remain unbetrothed, and even if he had, things were as he had feared; news of his upcoming nuptials were already being celebrated in the Kingdom.

"Son, you have given enough of your excuses over the years. This time circumstances are out of your control! The girl has been compromised."

Enlin crossed his arms and glared at Telphee. "She was not compromised! What was I to do, leave her standing outside of the door to freeze to death? I was a perfect gentleman. Phee could have left well enough alone."

Telphee poured more ale into his mug. "My first duty is to the King, and if the King wishes a bride for his son, then a bride he shall have. I saw an opportunity and I took it." He raised the mug and saluted Enlin with a mocking smirk.

"With little thought of the full perspective," Enlin tossed back. "You asked no questions and cared not at all of her status, and now a woman who seems to belong nowhere, and could be part of some plot to fell the Kingdom, is being forced upon me as a bride!"

"Your Majesty, I have already set the wedding preparations in motion. Word has been sent to the surrounding Kingdoms, but we needn't wait. If a plot has been thrust upon us, the wedding should commence immediately before time for a full launch has passed."

The King ran his hands through his already mussed hair. It had been a stressful night and morning for him. His son's marriage would happen. The mysterious lineage of the woman would have perhaps concerned him more if he did not have the recent missive that had been brought to him in the early hours of dawn to think of.

He had allowed Enlin far too much time to dally on an issue that should not have allowed leeway. Now, if war was upon them and something were to happen to his only son, there was no heir.

He cared not at all about his son's commitment issues. He himself had suffered a loveless marriage for years until the birth of his youngest had take the Queen from him. One did not marry for love if your blood was royal. It was duty that dictated the choice.

"I agree that a fortnight should be enough time. See that it is done, Telphee. Having all our allies here all at once leaves our outlying lands vulnerable. Those of the aristocracy that cannot make such a short time frame will have to be happy with joining in our celebration after it is done. Our scouts can alert us of impending arrivals, and we will accommodate with extended festivities and feasts."

"Very good, Your Majesty."

The King waved a hand, signaling that he was done with the discussion and Telphee rose to leave.

Enlin waited only for the door to close before turning to his father. "I cannot marry this woman!"

"Why?" his father demanded. "Is there some fact that you have neglected to share with me about her?"

"Yes!" Enlin had no choice. He would have to tell his father everything. It was the only way to stop it. "She spoke prophecy when she said the Kingdom would fall. If I marry her, it will."

"You're making no sense!" the King exploded. "Stop with all of your excuses! You will marry her. I will not be persuaded by arguments that have no gain!"

"Father, you do not understand! On the eve of my crowning, I left the castle. I met a sorceress who spoke things to me." Enlin stood in front of the King and grasped his arms. "Father, the woman told me that if I ever married, the Kingdom would fall."

"And what did she ply you with first? An unknown woman speaking nonsense is not something you stake your future on. Especially when one is a Prince."

The King was furious that he had never pressed deeper for his son's reasons for not finding a bride. If this was all it had been, he could have pressed for resolution sooner.

Enlin shook his head and dropped his arms. "She plied me with nothing. I was sober and alone. She spoke of things that she could not have known."

His father arched a brow.

"My birth. She said that I almost died. That the Queen had reasons for wanting me to and expressed her wish verbally that it would have been better if I had."

Enlin saw the truth of it in the eyes that looked back at him.

There was sorrow and anger. "This sorceress, did she have eyes like the sky and hair like the sun?"

The night was as fresh in Enlin's mind as though it had happened yesterday. His father's depiction of the woman was accurate. "How could you know this?"

The King had his own memories that lurked vividly. The night his firstborn son had been born was one of them. He had waited the long night for word of his son's fate. "That woman knew of your birth because she was there. There is no curse upon you. Nothing at all will happen if you marry."

Turning his eyes to one of the woven tapestries upon the wall, the King thought of the woman he had given no thought to at all in years. "That woman knew that she had no future with me. Your mother's jealousy raged. I was unaware of the lies that were spoken to your mother. The sorceress you speak of spread poison for years to your mother against both you and me."

Enlin was still reeling from his father's admission that he had been unfaithful. He had given no thought to the way his parents had felt about each other. He had been young when his mother had died and had only a few memories that he could recall. Most of his younger years had been spent in the care of servants.

The King did not often speak of his mother and Enlin had never asked questions.

"You had an affair with a sorceress?"

Enlin had believed the woman, completely. She had not seemed slighted but had been very serious. There had been a gleam of truth in her eyes that had made them a vivid blue that had seemed depthless. Could he have mistaken her behavior and words? Had she been delusional?

He did not like that he as suddenly questioning what he

had believed for years. Was he such a fool that h.
taken in so easily?

"She was not, and is not, a sorceress. She is just a woman.
I did not love the Queen, and I am but a man. Your mother
did not love me either, son, but still, she scorned me for my
mistresses."

"More than one?" Startled, Enlin stepped back from his
father. He knew his father was not perfect, but he had been
raised morally and with honor and been taught that those
qualities should extend into every part of one's life.

Vows, whether the one beside you had been chosen or
not, were sacred. Love or not, marriage meant two became
one, and nothing but God was meant to divide such a union.

A knock on the door held both of their tongues. The
butler opened it at the King's call. "Breakfast awaits, Your
Majesty. Shall I bring a tray for you?"

The King shook his head. "No. Our business here is
done." He waved a hand toward the door and Enlin had no
choice but to precede him. The King deemed the conversation over, but he was reeling. He had known nothing of the
past his father had spoken of.

Despite his father's words, he believed the prophecy still.
Unrest curled in his belly. There was far more to the story
than his father had told him. He would find the woman and
question her further. Perhaps the years would give him
better insight into her motives for what she had spoken
to him.

He could not leave it as it was. His mind was lurching
with demands for clarity. He had done what he thought best
for his Kingdom, for his people. For himself. Everything he
loved was at stake.

The words of the King were not enough for him to cast
aside a prophecy, that if true, would be the end of all he had
ever known.

CHAPTER 6

*H*is betrothed looked rested and well. Her hair had been brushed and braided back away from her face, making her golden eyes seem larger. Enlin took the seat beside her and found it oddly captivating that she did not smile and simper at him as so many of the nobility did when in attendance.

Rather, she looked at him as though she could see affliction in his eyes. "Do you see the demise of all that is around you again today?" he asked, leaning close so that only she could hear.

"Today I am pondering what it is to be..."

She seemed perplexed at what exactly it was she was striving for. Her last word held and then faded.

"Normal?" he supplied.

Her eyes slid away to study each of the serving maids hurrying around the room. "Are they normal?" she asked.

"If they are, you are not like them," Enlin replied dryly. Did she have no idea how different she was from anyone he had ever met? Her innocence was one thing, but it was the way that she saw what was around her that made her stand out. There were many women that were beautiful and graceful, but though he tried, he could think of none that seemed to look beyond the surface as she did.

"Should I be?" she inquired further.

Enlin could not help but laugh. Even the things she spoke aloud set her apart. No other woman would ask such things. "No. You're far more interesting as you are."

"But how does one be anything at all if they know nothing of themselves?"

It was an excellent question. And one he did not have an answer for. Enlin supposed that it would be difficult to go about your daily life with no recollection of what ordinarily happened. He thought of how he would feel in such a situation as he ate his bread and drank his wine.

His sisters were not in attendance, which was typical of them. They both liked to sleep until the day neared the supper hour. He wondered how they would receive Breeon.

The eldest of the two, Kahlee, was spoiled and he doubted she would look kindly upon anyone who would dare to take even the smallest bit of attention off of her. She had just become of age and was enjoying the stream of suitors who were vying for her hand.

Nyala was quiet and Enlin doubted she would say much at all, as was customary for her. He worried often for his youngest sister. She despised being the forefront of anything and he had defended her honor more than once when she had failed to speak out of fright or shyness and been deemed simple.

He guessed that he was closest to her of anyone, if only because he had always fiercely protected her. Thinking of her gave him his answer for Breeon.

"You should be what you feel you are and nothing else," he said, giving his full attention back to the woman at his side.

"Lost then?" she responded with a quirk of her lips. "The

hallways of this castle are a mirror of the maze in my mind. Difficult to navigate and full of dead ends."

Enlin chuckled. "There are no dead ends in the castle, Lady Breeon."

"That is not true. I came upon a wall this morning that seemed to have no reason to be there at all."

"Where was your servant? You should not wander the castle alone."

"If you mean Velynn, the girl who has been helping me since I arrived, that is where she found me."

Glancing at each of the servants Enlin realized he knew none of them by name. "I have no idea who you speak of." Each of their attendants were present, waiting until they were needed, helping with the duties of serving breakfast. As a future Princess, it would not be allowed that only servants continue to attend to her.

"Velynn has been very helpful."

Protocol dictated his next words would be true even if he or she wanted a different outcome. "As my betrothed, Ladies of nobility shall attend to you. The servants are temporary."

"I cannot marry you, so it is not necessary."

Enlin lifted a hand to quiet her. "Lady Breeon, be mindful of your words," he warned quietly, leaning in again. To anyone observing they would be nothing more than the couple they were supposed to be portraying. "I seek to avoid the marriage myself, but we cannot speak of it here."

The third course of the meal was served. Nuts, cheese, and spiced wine. Enlin needed to understand why she was insisting that they could not marry. Could it be possible that the same sorceress had spoken a prophecy to her?

"The fountain is beautiful in the west courtyard," he said conversationally. "Join me there as the sun sets and we can speak again."

They would not be overheard there, and a chaperone could hover at the edges. It would further cement the illusion of the betrothal, but Enlin had few other options for speaking to her privately.

Enlin spent his afternoon in the presence of the Royal Council. There was much discussion to be had with the sudden arrival of a wedding. Because Breeon's nobility had not been established, messengers had been sent to the bordering aristocracy searching for her identity, as well as to all the surrounding Kingdoms, in the hopes that they would find her lineage.

There was plenty of advice given on how to handle the situation from the Council and opposing sides for the union sparked more than one heated argument. Enlin did not voice any of his opinions on the matter. It would not do for anyone in the Kingdom to know that he objected to the marriage, not only for Breeon's sake if the union took place, but for peace among the people. Any division at all was a seed of doubt he did not want planted.

It was always better to present a united front when a decision affected the whole of the Kingdom, and a Princess in line to be Queen would impact his people. There had been no Queen for so long that many had forgotten what good one could bring to the Kingdom.

Enlin knew the role Breeon could play. He had listened to more than one lecture from his father over the value of taking a wife. Besides the all-important role of providing an heir, she could take on roles of charity among the peasants, and further deepen their relationships with the royals among other bloodlines.

His personal perspective of the neighboring royal and noble wives was one of secrets and lies, clandestine affairs, and politics. Power and money without morality and honor made people heartless and cruel. Or bored.

Once he had considered what he would want for a wife, and it had not been anything like the version status seemed to dictate. He much preferred the contrast he had seen within the peasant homes he had visited. From what he could tell, the peasant husbands and wives actually seemed to like each other.

It had been in those same homes that he had told himself repeatedly that he could never have what they had. It was for the people that he had made his choice to make sure he never fulfilled the prophecy that would take the peace his Kingdom enjoyed.

Enlin had heard tales of war. War was not something he wanted on his lands. He did not want to lose his men to battle or force the women and children to flee for their own safety. They had never needed to defend the castle walls in his or his father's lifetime, and he had never forgotten the lessons his grandfather had spoken to him before he had died.

The Council finally broke for supper. The hall was filled with aristocracy and peasants come to offer congratulations and get a look at Breeon. As was tradition, for supper the women sat separately as the King listened to news and other matters.

His sisters were both in attendance. Kahlee sat amongst a gathering of noble wives, and Nyala sat at the end of the long table, head down and silent. From his observations, Breeon was immersed in dealing with the women who had settled themselves by her. He could not tell if she was handling it well.

Supper tended to be a long affair, and for the King could last for hours depending on the number of issues being brought before him. The women had long vacated the hall before Enlin was able to rise and seek out the patter of falling water from one level to another.

Enlin had always loved the west fountain. He had a few favored places in the castle, but outdoors this fountain was his favorite; a depiction of a Lion guarding his cubs, its mouth open in a roar. Despite the cold, no fresh snow had fallen.

Enlin doubted that they would see much more snow. The season was almost over, and spring would break forth soon enough.

Breeon sat on an area of the white wall that surrounded the glistening water. The cloak that had shrouded her for the ride to the castle had been replaced with a rich white one that spilled around her like a fresh fall of snow that had wanted only to be in her presence.

"Lady Breeon, forgive me for making you wait."

"I am told I am to address you as Prince Enlin, or Your Highness, or I am being disrespectful."

Enlin sat. "Were the ladies of the court kind to you?"

"I'm afraid I may have asked too many questions. One of them told me I was a 'curious thing.' Am I curious Prince Enlin?"

"Yes," Enlin said without hesitation. "I would guess that the Ladies did not mean it in a nice way?"

The Prince watched Breeon run her finger over the stone of the ledge they sat upon. "I think that I was 'curious' before..."

"Have you remembered something, Lady Breeon?"

She lifted her eyes and in the fading light, it was as though the surface of the water glimmered there. "I didn't want you to think... I don't want you to think that I am a part of something that could hurt you or your Kingdom. So, I tried to remember."

Breeon looked out over the water. The sun was almost too low to see, and the water was shaded with yellows and soft pinks. Her past was never far from her mind and because she was only thinking about that, she did not see the Prince as he looked upon her face, waiting for her to confirm that she was not the threat that half the council believed that she was.

Prince Enlin, for just a few moments, allowed himself to consider a future with her. One where it was his role to protect her, not only from the Ladies who used their nobility to treat others whatever way they liked, but from everything, no matter the circumstances.

"I cannot tell you who I am more than my name." Breeon reached out and tentatively touched the Prince's arm, then pulled back when deep inside of her, something flashed to life. A yearning that she did not understand.

In her eyes, light sparked, golden flecks that burned to life for only seconds, but it was enough for her to remember that she was not normal and that she could not marry the man who sat in front of her, questioning who she really was. And deep inside of her, a soft familiar melody vibrated a song until her anxiety hushed it away.

CHAPTER 7

*B*reeon stood, feeling unsettled as the faint chords faded. "I cannot marry you, Prince Enlin. It is forbidden. It matters not what it means for my future. It simply cannot happen." She wandered away down the stone path, needing distance between them.

"This is not the first time that you have stated that you can not marry me, but why this time do you say it is forbidden?" Falling into step beside her, Enlin knew that it wasn't fair for him to feel a twinge when she said it, when he himself had told her the exact same thing from the beginning, but he didn't like that she was opposed to the idea.

"You continue to ask me for answers that I cannot supply. I feel it, strongly. Enough to know that I need to listen."

"And what happens if neither one of us can prevent this marriage from happening, Lady Breeon?" For him, the consequences could take everything that he had ever known. For her, she spoke from nothing but her heart leading her. For that reason, the sting was sharper to him. It felt personal.

Whatever her reason, Enlin realized that her belief in the words she spoke was as real to her as his belief in the words the sorceress had spoken. Was it coincidence that the path life had placed them on had led them both to the same conclusion?

The magnitude of the realization made Enlin pause. "We must stop it from happening." He faced her, blocking the stone path, thinking that if her eyes were a dull color, it would be so much easier to look into them. "Our goals are the same. There must be some way to prevent the marriage that will leave neither of us in ruin."

"I could leave. I never meant to become a burden to you when I stood before your door. I only sought the warmth of your fire."

"And where would you go, Lady Breeon? You remember no home, no family. You had nothing with you. I am afraid that without my protection, your future would be bleak."

"I could serve as Velynn does."

Enlin scoffed. "A castle servant? Lady Breeon, you are no servant. Your blood is as noble as the aristocracy. I would bet on it, despite your lack of knowledge on your lineage."

"If life dictates that I must serve others to prevent..."

He watched her try to gather her thoughts. Frustration gathered in the gold flecks in her eyes, darkening them.

Enlin reached out to take her hand in his. Her skin was cold, but so soft. "Someone will know who you are. Please do not fret. We have sent messengers throughout the land to find where you belong."

They would find nothing. Breeon knew the truth as she looked back at him. She did not belong. The why was absent, but she knew it was the truth. What did that mean for her? If she could not marry the Prince, and she had nowhere to go and no other options, what exactly was she meant to do?

Needing the comfort his strong hand gave, she closed her fingers around his, finding the touch pleasant. "And if they do not, Prince Enlin, what happens to me then?"

"Perhaps the answers both of us seek are not here." Letting go of her hand, Enlin took a step back. Her fingers had warmed in his grasp and the thought that he would not mind having the right to hold her hand whenever he liked was disturbing. It was never good to want something that you could not have.

He had one plan. To seek the sorceress who had spoken his fate in the first place to hopefully uncover more. Leading the way back to the castle, Enlin thought again about how to go about finding the woman from his past. He knew nothing about her and the long ago meeting itself had been a chance encounter, as far as he knew. The likelihood of finding her at all was slim.

In the morning, he decided that he would take Rylan and they would embark on a search. But first, he would visit with someone who might know the identity of the woman he sought.

He bid Breeon a good night at the castle doors that opened out into the yard.

It was late, but he would seek his answers now. Once, the Queen had commanded multitudes of servants, but Enlin remembered only one who might remember anything from his own birth.

The late hour was in his favor. Enlin changed his cloak for one of lesser finery and left the castle through one of the servant halls that was rarely used.

Theara had been one of his mother's servants before and after his birth. He had few memories of her left, but they were fond. She had told him stories and rocked him as a child, and it had been her that had made him feel loved.

Enlin had a strong recollection of his mother finding him a nuisance and her Ladies-in-waiting had treated him much the same. It made far more sense now that he knew part of the story surrounding his birth.

He hadn't realized until the dots started to connect that she had probably been dismissed when his mother had died. Enlin had seen Theara over the years in the village market and knew that she had a family of her own and seemed well.

Unsure of how he would be received, Enlin knocked at her door and waited. She opened the door herself and he watched surprise cover her face that quickly turned to delight as she curtsied. "Prince Enlin! Welcome! Please, please, come in!" She stepped back and allowed him entry, closing the door and rushing to move to another doorway where she quietly murmured to someone beyond before turning back to him.

"Would you like to sit, Prince Enlin?" she asked, indicating a chair.

"I need to speak to you privately, Theara, if that is possible?"

"Whatever you wish, Prince Enlin. Allow me to serve tea and I will send everyone away?"

"Thank you, Theara." Enlin chose a chair at the table and waved to another, trying to put her at ease. He could see her anxiety at his unexpected presence. She sat at his gesture, perched on the edge, her gaze curious, her fingers wrapping around each other tightly.

"Your family is well?"

"They are yes, Prince Enlin. Thank you for asking."

A young girl with similar features to Theara's came out with a tray, a blush staining her cheeks as she set it down carefully. She then dropped into an awkward curtsy.

"Thank you, Lianna. The Prince needs to speak with me. Please take your brother and join your father until I come for you." The girl obeyed immediately and Theara poured the tea, adding one spoonful of sugar at his request.

"How can I help you, Prince Enlin?" Theara handed him his cup of tea and offered the small plate of biscuits her daughter had also placed on the tray.

"I have recently discovered that there were circumstances

that I was unaware of surrounding my birth and I need some answers. You were there?"

She nodded in affirmation. "What is it that you would like to know?"

Enlin had not missed the subtle shift of her body in the chair or the nervous clatter of her cup on the saucer. "There was a woman there. I need to learn her identity."

"There were many women attending to your mother."

He knew that she stalled. He had only to determine why, and he would have the information he sought. "You know the woman I speak of. She was the King's mistress."

Enlin expected shock; instead, sorrow filled Theara's eyes. She rose abruptly and moved to the window, swishing the curtain aside to look out. He watched her as she walked to each of the doors that led out of the room before returning to her seat.

"Prince Enlin." She leaned forward and took his hand, her eyes earnest. "There are some things that should be left well enough alone."

"You needn't worry about sparing my feelings. I am no longer a boy, and the answers that I seek are for far greater reasons than easing my curiosity."

She searched his eyes, and Enlin wondered what it was she wanted to see. He was unsure if she saw what she hoped, but resignation tightened her lips, and she leaned back heavily against her chair and let out a long sigh.

"You understand the things you are asking for could mean my death?"

"Your death?" Enlin had not expected those words. His heart beat faster in his chest. What secrets ran through his Kingdom that threatened the stability and peace his father had worked so hard to build?

Her voice was hushed when she began to speak. Enlin had to lean forward to hear her. "The woman you seek was banished. She was your father's mistress, yes, but it was not to slight your mother. She was here to protect your mother, and you, but the King wanted more than that."

Their tea was forgotten, cooling beside them as quickly as the illusion he had held of what his Kingdom was. Enlin nodded for her to continue.

"Your birth was vital, Enlin. You were to be the only male heir and your mother knew that. She did everything in her power not to become pregnant, but she failed. You were destined to be born."

This was far more than he had thought to learn. He had wanted only a name and Theara was weaving a story of treason and secrecy. "Why would my mother not want an heir? As the Queen, she would have known how important it was."

Theara's eyes traveled around the room to each window and door again and when she spoke this time, her words were little more than a whisper. "Your mother was a traitor, Prince Enlin. Her death was no accident. Her death was meant to save your life."

Enlin pushed back in his chair and stood up, walking away from the fragments of the truth that he had held before Theara had torn it to pieces. What more did he not know? Could he handle more? His mind was whirling with everything he had just been told, trying to separate it into something that made sense.

Except none of it did. He had wanted Theara to tell him the same thing his father had. That the woman had been no more than a jilted lover and there were no consequences awaiting his upcoming marriage.

Now, more than ever, he had no choice but to find the woman. He wanted to know exactly what she had known all those years ago when she had warned him that his future was not meant for the path that would inevitably be laid out for him.

Facing Theara, he asked for the woman's name.

Her lips tightened again, and she gave a slight shake of her head.

"You don't know, or you won't tell me?"

"Please, Prince Enlin, tell me why it is so important for you to know? I should not tell you."

Knowing he must be as mindful as her about listening ears, Enlin returned to the chair and sat again. "I met her once, years ago. She told me if I ever married, the Kingdom would fall. She told me a tale of death and sorrow that would destroy the peace that we enjoy now. She said that everything would change, and it would never be gained again if I did not listen."

Understanding spread over Theara's face. "Ahh. I have heard of your betrothal. I was unaware that you carried your own secret." Her head lowered and he watched her turn her hands palms up and look at them for a few moments before she lifted her head again and gave him what he had sought. "Her name is Alayna."

Theara took one of the Prince's hands in both of hers. "You deserve happiness, my Prince. I know that you feel the fate of the Kingdom rests on you. There are many secrets that flow beneath the surface. I hope that the answers that you seek can give you the freedom to find love and live out your days in peace."

The look on her face contradicted her hope for him, but there was sincerity in the words.

Enlin squeezed the hands that held his and stood. "Thank you for speaking with me. I know that I can trust you with everything that has been said here. May I reward your kindness with a gift?"

"Go in peace, Prince Enlin. We have everything we need."

CHAPTER 8

*I*n the morning, Enlin wasted no time gathering what he would need for the journey. As his most trusted friend, he woke Rylan at dawn and explained shortly his intent. With nary a word, Rylan packed his own bag and followed Enlin to the waiting horses.

The stable boy stifled a yawn as he handed up the reins. He had been startled awake at Enlin's hand on his shoulder so early but had jumped up to do the Prince's bidding.

Enlin had not chosen his normal stallion. The last thing he wanted was to draw attention. Rylan was accompanying him not only for protection, but to ease the lecture he knew he would receive upon his return. Leaving without an entourage of soldiers around him would not make the King happy. Peace did not mean leaving oneself vulnerable.

With only a partial plan in place, they rode hard throughout the morning until they reached their first destination. Rylan had kept pace, and his silence, as they had traveled, but questioned the Prince as he swung down from his horse. "Need I be on guard, Prince? Who hails here and what business do we have?"

"A friend hails here. He will accompany us on our journey

and will be our face for questions. I have no desire to arouse suspicion."

"And when will you share your purpose for this sudden crusade we have embarked upon?" No one waited in the small stable for their horses, so they were securing them themselves.

Settled with water and feed, they left the stables. A man with sword at side made his way toward them. Enlin grinned and lifted a hand. "I will tell you both together," he assured and stopped to wait. It would be better to speak away from the house.

"Weston!" he greeted when the man drew close.

"Your Highness! This is a surprise!" Weston nodded at Rylan and drew up alongside them. "Please, come to the house and I shall prepare a proper welcome."

"No need," Enlin discouraged. "I need to speak with you and here will do."

"Of course," Weston acknowledged. "What is it that I can do for you, Prince Enlin?"

The Prince explained his mission shortly to both. "I seek a woman from my boyhood. She spoke a warning to me that I took very seriously at the time but has since come to light as possibly false. Until I know for sure, I must proceed believing that it could be true for the sake of the Kingdom."

"A threat, Prince? You did not speak of this to me!" Rylan was clearly displeased. "We could have dealt with this accordingly if you had only told me!"

Enlin shook his head. "I spoke of it to no one, Rylan. You needn't be so indignant. As a boy, I settled what I was told in the back of my mind. As a man, it has lurked but was not quite as important as it has suddenly become."

"What exactly did this threat regard?"

"It was not a threat; it was a warning."

Rylan crossed his arms. "You are being far too vague, Prince. I must demand more information."

Weston had stayed quiet, but his expression as the Prince had spoken had stayed grim. "Does this have anything to do with your recent betrothal, Prince Enlin?"

"You have heard already?"

The corners of Weston's mouth curved slightly. "I doubt there is anyone within the Kingdom who has not, Prince. It is the juiciest bit of gossip in years, as my wife has declared many a time in the past days."

"It has only become news recently. Telphee has done his job well." Enlin was annoyed. If everyone knew of his upcoming nuptials it would be that much harder to put an end to them. "Yes, the warning does pertain to the marriage. I was warned all those years ago that marrying would bring about the fall of the Kingdom."

Both men regarded Enlin blankly at this announcement. Rylan spoke first. "Prince Enlin, forgive me, but the ramblings of a... random woman, perhaps should not be taken seriously. It would not be the first time that lies were whispered to one containing royal blood."

"The woman was nothing to me. A chance meeting upon the road. Nor do I believe she spoke lies. There was truth in her words, and I must now find her to discover what prompted her to speak the warning. I believe that she may know more than she voiced."

"Rylan is right, my Prince. Unless she was a sorceress, if one believes in such things, how could she possibly believe an event such as a marriage could cause the destruction of anything, except of course peace of mind." The last Weston added with a wry quirk of mouth and a glance back toward his home behind him.

Enlin could not help but grin. He knew Weston well enough to know that his marriage was a happy one, and his wife was not the quiet sort who held her tongue.

"I applaud both of you for offering sound arguments, but

I simply cannot discard the words. There seems to be more at play."

Summarizing the strange encounter between the King and Breeon only increased the skepticism on Rylan's strong features. He was shaking his head by the end. "Prince Enlin, a conspiracy could very well be at play here. While the woman seems innocent enough, you must admit that how she came to be in your presence at such a time, with no memory, is concerning? All of this could be a ploy for your affections to bring down the Kingdom."

"No," Enlin disagreed strongly. "She is not a part of it. She does not wish to marry me."

"You know as well as I that she has no choice but to marry you! It cannot be stopped without her ruin or her death." Rylan began to pace, muttering as he did so.

"It was Telphee who demanded we go to the cabin to see of your safety. Could he have something to do with this?"

"Phee?" Enlin laughed. "Rylan, you are speaking nonsense." He left Rylan to his ramblings and gave his attention to his friend. "You both know the situation now. Weston, will you accompany us? We need a face that can quietly make inquiries that will be forgotten as soon as the question is over."

Weston lifted both brows and smirked. "Why Prince, how gracious of you to say! I know that I am common, but I was unaware of my seeming insignificance."

Enlin grinned. "With all due respect, I only meant that as you are not a royal, your questions will not become fodder for conspiracy or gossip."

Weston was laughing and Enlin was glad that no offense had really been taken. "Relax, Prince Enlin, my wife stokes my ego enough that I need not your approval. Of course, I will go. Saddle a horse for me, won't you Rylan, while I say good-bye to my wife?"

Rylan waved a hand in dismissal and turned back into the

stable with pursed lips and tightly drawn in brows. "Prince Enlin, I have no idea how you intend to find this woman, and even if we do, how do you think she can prove such a thing?"

"My instinct tells me this is what I have to do," Enlin explained. He had little hope that he could say anything that would appease Rylan's distress. "You have always trusted my instincts before."

"Your instincts have never revolved around a woman before," Rylan said drily. "Women always seem to muddle things up."

Rylan had long been one of his men to avoid female companionship and had often scoffed at how easily men fell prey to a pretty smile or a flutter of lashes. Enlin remembered an evening of merriment, celebrating a noble wedding in a bordering Kingdom that had led to him reprimanding Rylan for a strongly declared comment that the groom was a fool.

Many noble weddings were often arranged, but this one had been a union requested for the reason of love and granted for political favor.

Enlin had not held the same opinion Rylan had as he had watched the faces of the bride and groom as they pledged their lives to each other. He had wondered if the groom saw the adoration in the eyes of his bride and thought that perhaps it would be comforting to know that someone cared so deeply about you.

But what had he known of love then, or even now? Nothing. He had never had the love of a mother or of any woman. The King saw him in good favor and respected him, but Enlin had never heard him utter words of love. Love was as foreign to him as the Kingdom.

The tales had been passed down through the centuries, rooted in messages of love. Steeped in impossibility, they spoke of creatures fallen to earth to save the soul of a mere human. There were many versions and many tales, but all of them touted selfless acts of love that accomplished ๖ things and changed the lives of many.

Enlin's favorite had always been of the creature who fell and lost his golden powers to take up a sword and fight a mighty battle against a monster meant to devour all and leave the world devoid of humanity.

With incredible strength and courage, the creature had risen among the men of the earth and fought for them, and with them, striking down the enemies that had been called forth by the monster to slaughter them.

Even with great odds against them, the creature had sung, his deep voice filling the air with a cry for the powers of heaven to aid them.

The battle had been long and bloody, but the creature never mysterious creatures of gold that abounded within the legends of the faltered.

He had ended it with his sword through the heart of the monster, and then he had fallen to his knees and the harmony of his song had changed, making all who heard weep at the plea from his soul.

His song had been one of faith and mercy, and a glory that could not be bound, and the creature had lifted his arms and gold dust had begun to fall around him, coating his skin. It had been blinding in its brightness until for a long while, the air and sky had been filled with it so that all had to close their eyes against the brilliance.

When it had faded, the creature had been gone, and those that had witnessed the wonder of it had no longer been sure if the creature had ever been there or not.

The tale came to him as Weston returned and they mounted their horses to begin their quest. Enlin had always hoped that he had some of the same courage inside of him that the tale spoke of. That had been one of his greatest desires since he had heard the tale as a young child.

CHAPTER 9

"*A* good cup of ale is the best way to gain information, Prince," Weston told him as they rested their horses outside of the town Enlin had visited long ago.

Armed with only a first name and the description the King had used of her, Weston planned to ply for information about the woman with drink. He was not known in the town and would arouse no suspicion asking after a woman.

Weston's ability to use words to his advantage had been why Enlin had chosen him. They had been friends since childhood and had embarked on more than one adventure that had ended with Weston using his gift to explain their escapades as nothing more than boyhood play.

"What will you do if you discover nothing, Prince Enlin? It is possible that this woman will not be found."

"Let's try having a positive outlook, shall we Rylan?" Enlin could not think about failing. His Kingdom was at stake. His people's livelihoods. Perhaps even his life and that of his fathers.

"We will find her," Weston exclaimed. "You can speak with her and put this falsity to rest, marry your betrothed, and live happily ever after!"

"How very optimistic of you," Rylan said with a frown. "It would be better to prepare ourselves for all possible outcomes so that we can be prepared with how to proceed next if need be."

"Nevertheless, I hope to make my Prince happy by returning with the information we seek." Weston turned his horse and with a nod, urged his horse into a gallop.

Enlin hoped as he watched his friend put distance between them that his confidence would pay off.

Still, as he and Rylan sat around a fire later waiting for Westons return he could not stop his mind from seizing on the anxiety of how little time he had to accomplish the deed he had set for himself. And what of Breeon's own statement that she herself could not marry?

Even if he were able to cast aside the prophecy spoken over himself, what of hers? What secret did her mind hold that made her speak of her own inability to join her life with another?

Had he lived all his life with the illusion of peace? The secrets that had overtaken the relative calm of his Princely days were gnawing at him. Did his father live with such things weighing on him?

Enlin had not given much time to thinking about the things that his father had experienced or how the events of his father's own life had made him who he was. He had done what he could to please his father, learning the art of sword-fighting, the strategies of war, the politics of peace, and every other thing that pertained to ruling a Kingdom. Had it been enough?

Had he been selfish? Personal conversations about thoughts and feelings had just not been commonplace. Enlin imagined they would have been awkward had they tried.

He had known his grandfather for only a short time. His grandfather had been frail and withered from his life, but Enlin had often sat by his bedside as a child and listened to the stories of war and division that had plagued the Kingdoms during his reign.

He had no recollection of who the man had been other when he had been well enough to grace the throne. His father had commented many times that he had wanted to be a different kind of King.

The unrest in the Kingdom had not begun during his grandfather's reign, but from what Enlin understood, the former King had fed off the power struggle and deemed himself worthy of more power, wealth, and adoration.

When Enlin's father had taken the throne, the Kingdom had breathed in relief at the news that their new King wanted peace.

It was admirable that it had been accomplished. It had taken nearly two decades, but eventually the bloodshed had ceased.

His grandfather had died proclaiming that it was not possible and ridiculing his son for his unrealistic ideals.

Enlin respected his father for never backing down on his stance. He had done everything in his power to bring peace to the people. How could one fault a man for such a thing?

The determination and disciple it must have taken to pursue peace year after year had earned his father a great deal of respect, not just from his son.

Enlin realized that perhaps he had put his father up on a pedestal. One that had shaken when he had heard of the infidelities of the past.

Would the knowledge he was seeking change his view of his father even more? Of the Kingdom he would rule one day?

He needed to also consider what good it would do for him as a King if no heir was ever produced? There was that problem he had yet to consider if he took no bride.

His sister could be Queen upon his death, of course, but the history of past Queens that he had been taught had spoken of uprisings of political conflict and attempts at war until either the Queen had married and given the Kingdom a King or died. Unfair, but he would not wish such strife upon either of his sisters.

Annoyed that his thoughts had taken such a cynical path, Enlin stood to fetch the kettle to heat water. Like his father, he had always wanted the peace and comfort that blessed the land. That passion, at least, he could credit the King for.

Beyond that, his perspective had widened considerable in the last few days. What more could he do for the Kingdom with a Queen by his side? Could a Queen accomplish things that he could not? The people were used to seeing the empty throne beside their King. He wondered now how the Queen's death had affected them.

"Rylan, do you remember my mother?"

"I do, yes."

"Was she loved by the people?"

Rylan hesitated. "Why do you ask, Prince Enlin?"

"My mind contemplates things I have never given thought to before."

"Because of Lady Breeon?"

"Because of the marriage," Enlin corrected. He knew barely anything about the woman currently slated to be his bride. She couldn't possibly be affecting his thoughts.

"I don't wish to speak ill of anyone, Prince. The Queen is gone now."

Sitting cross-legged on his fur on the ground, Enlin rested an arm on a knee. "A Queen could further strengthen the Kingdom."

"Unless it falls as has been predicted, you mean," Rylan countered.

"If that is proved to be false, perhaps taking a bride would be good. I should pose the question to Weston's wife. Hear her thoughts on it outside of the gossip aspect."

"These questions have nothing to do with Lady Breeon? Are you taken with her Prince Enlin?"

Enlin frowned at Rylan. "I've just told you that I barely know her."

"She is beautiful."

"Beauty fades. If one is drawn in by only that, what is left when it is gone or the infatuation wanes?"

Rylan nodded his agreement and gave Enlin a sympathetic look. "Your mother."

"Pardon?"

"Forgive me, Prince Enlin, but if you want the truth, your mother was not loved. She was bitter, entitled, and jealous. Once, your father looked upon her favorably because she was beautiful, but after she became his bride, he discovered that she cared little about the things he felt were important. It is good that you see past the surface of things. That has always been one of your strengths."

"It is nice of you to say so, but I am beginning to believe that I have been very selfish. I have sought the solitude of the cabin many times to escape from my duties, frustrated at their toll on me. Perhaps I should have been more focused on how I could change things for the better."

"That has always been your goal, Prince. Your path has not been misdirected." Rylan's voice was kind.

"When it suited me." Enlin took hold of the steaming kettle with a cloth and added water to the cups Rylan had set out. "I fear that I will have to choose one demise over the other. Lady Breeon's or the Kingdoms."

"I have not meant to be discouraging, Prince Enlin. I seek only to offer wise counsel, but I want only what is best for all involved. We will find a way to maintain peace."

"I hope you are right, Rylan. For all our sakes, I pray for a favorable outcome."

Enlin considered pressing for more information about

his mother, but he had not been able to come to terms with what he had already learned.

Knowing his mother had found his presence a nuisance was far different than knowing she had wanted him dead.

His tea was too hot to drink. Enlin cradled the mug in his hands, watching the steam snake into the air.

"We've never spoken of your own parents. Where are they, Rylan?"

A shoulder lifted in response. "They aren't worth a conversation."

Rylan had watched over him for as long as Enlin could remember. He had been the one to teach him to ride, to hold and use a sword, and how to engage in hand-to-hand combat.

There were not many years between them, but as Enlin regarded

Rylan across the fire, he realized in a way, Rylan had far more of a father than his own. It was Rylan he sought out when he needed to talk, to escape or needed answers.

"Are they gone?"

Rylan looked out into the fading light around them, his jaw tightening. "No."

It seemed Rylan did not want to give more and Enlin did not want to press. He had thought only to find out more about the man who was so constantly by his side. Yet one more lapse on his part that he had failed to notice. He disliked that he had been far more focused on his own life than he had once thought.

"My mother was a fool that believed in fairy tales," Rylan said abruptly. "My father, well, I'll just say he didn't give me much to use to view him in a favorable light."

"I'm sorry, Rylan."

Rylan took a cautious sip of his tea. "God willing, you learn from your parents' mistakes. I tried to. I avoid drink, I avoid women, and I don't believe in fairy tales."

Enlin had never viewed Rylan as a jaded person, but perhaps he was wrong. "So, you've determined to be alone for the rest of your life? I'm not sure that is the best way to interpret your past into your future. There are good women in this world."

"I have stood by your side often enough to witness far too many unhappy unions, Prince. That is not a life that I want."

"You're speaking of the aristocracy?" Enlin inquired. He set his still too-hot tea down and crossed his arms. "You cannot use those as your baseline. Many of those marriages were arranged.

You are free to choose your wife. Do you not believe that choice can create a far different outcome?"

Rylan took a sip from his mug, grimacing when the heat scalded his lips and tongue. "No."

"Weston is happy," Enlin pointed out.

The look the Prince received indicated Rylan did not want to continue the conversation.

Sighing, Enlin let it go. He considered that he was deflecting; focusing on Rylan's future to avoid thinking about how much his would change if the marriage did happen. Marrying Breeon would be no different than an arranged marriage for him, as he knew nothing about her. It was too soon to conclude anything of her character or temperament, especially with the memory loss to consider.

Did losing one's view of oneself change the way you interacted with the world? Would she change once her memory returned?

He hoped not. He liked the sweetness about her and the way that she spoke the things that came into her mind. He appreciated the lack of guile when she smiled at him. He thought that perhaps he could be happy with Breeon as his wife. Except that she would not be.

Whatever hands of fate were at work had not blessed them to unite.

CHAPTER 10

"*P*rince Enlin, you set before yourself a monumental task!" Weston dismounted his horse, his feet thudding on the ground beside his prone companions.

Enlin was settled in his furs. The fire burned and darkness had fallen long ago. The night was chilly and quiet. It had been a while since Enlin had spent a night below the stars. "What do you have to report, Weston?"

Weston had pulled over the rolled fur they'd set out for him and was busy setting up a space of his own. "I had to imbibe in far more drink than my wife would be happy with. I turned my ear many times and spun my tale in seemingly endless ways, until finally I was rewarded with a tidbit that led me on a roundabout journey through the streets until I achieved the task set out for me by my Prince!"

Weston finished his story beneath the folds of his covers, his arms beneath his head, and a smile upon his face.

"You found the woman?"

"Ah, but I did not. Alas, she is shrouded in secrecy and tales that make the heart pitter patter. However, I believe I have a very good idea on where it is that she resides."

"Does your speech suggest she may be the sorceress I believe?"

"The consensus seems to agree. I, however, think that perhaps one that is different may be viewed in ways that do not give light to who they really are."

Enlin thought of Breeon. Was she as she seemed? An innocent woman who had lost her way, or a woman who was embedded in a sinister plot? It was difficult to determine if she was one or the other, and possible with her memory loss that she was both.

What had happened to her, Enlin wondered, not for the first time. Had she been alone, or had someone left her as she had been? Who would do such a thing? If she hadn't come across the cabin, the winter cold that had clung to her would have taken her. Of course, that led him back to it not being happenstance that she had come across the cabin.

"What is it that you think you have learned about the woman that we seek?"

Weston yawned and pulled his fur higher. "Ah, well one cannot say whether the tales I heard are truth or lie, but I have determined from the information that I collected that we will find her in the Woods Of Valoria. The townspeople fear her, although allegedly she hardly ever leaves whatever haven she calls her home, but it cannot be far as she frequents the town for her needs."

"Did they say what it is about her that instills fear?"

"I was told tales about visions that brought sorrow into the lives of many. It is said that she brings curses with her wherever she goes and that her soul is lost."

Enlin thought of the words that she had spoken to him. There had been such compassion in her eyes and an urgency in the way she had clasped his hands as she spoke her warning. He had felt no ill will directed toward him. Could one's soul be lost if you cared for their happiness?

"None of the things she spoke to people resulted in a

good outcome?" he inquired. "Perhaps her warnings were meant to save people from sorrow."

"Forgive me, Prince, for not having an answer for your question. I did not think to press for such details. I was told only of the distress her words have caused."

Enlin nodded in the firelight and closed his eyes. "We shall converse more in the morning, Weston. The night will begin to fade soon, and I am tired."

The words of others had no bearing on what had been spoken over him. Her warning had placed the choice in his hands. Had she given others a choice as well? Had they failed to heed caution and directly opposed her predictions? If they had, would that not mean that the fault lay with them and not with the woman?

It was possible she had the answers and knew if those that feared her had only defied what they had decided meant nothing.

The Woods of Valoria were not far. It was early afternoon the following day when they paused their horses to study the giant tangled trees that were indicative of the woods before them.

Many believed the trees themselves were cursed, and according to those who had dared to enter, the forest itself was a maze of limbs that twined around one another and made passage difficult.

Enlin had never gone into the woods himself. The tales attached to the trees were many, and Enlin realized as he looked at the twisted, dark trunks that perhaps he himself had believed the stories that they were haunted as well.

Trees were trees, he told himself as he urged his horse forward. He didn't believe in magic and sorcery. Not really. When he had questioned the identity of the woman who had given him his fate, she had replied that most knew her as a sorceress. He had not delved further for details as she had captured his attention with her plea that he must listen, and all but her foreboding premonition of his future had been forgotten.

"Surely no one lives here," Rylan commented. They had been forced to dismount their horses to lead them over the exposed roots and spreading branches obstructing any semblance of a path, twisting over, through and around each other exactly as described.

The Woods of Valoria became more mysterious the deeper they went. On the boundary of the wood, the leaves had been draped over and around the tall trunks in a deep shade of green that had given the illusion darkness clung to them. On the inside, the leaves began to change, the monotone green beginning to glisten with shimmers of color. Muted oranges and yellows, soft greens and whites, and vibrant shades of red, all that drew the eye and took mysterious to breathtaking.

"I do not feel comfortable here, Prince Enlin." Rylan stopped on the path and looked back at his Prince. The colors surrounding them did not put him at ease, but instead made him feel that it was possible the woman they sought was a sorceress after all.

Weston thought the forest fascinating and reflected that his wife would enjoy the beauty of it.

Enlin did as he always did when faced with a new situation and considered if there was anything of worth for his Kingdom and its people within the woods.

The obstructing roots and reaching branches that spread like tentacles were a hindrance to ease of movement, but he could well believe that many would find the coiling curves and arches beautiful. They had had to turn back to find another way again and again.

"We cannot stop, Rylan. If the lady resides within these woods, we will find her."

They were all reluctant to hack at the roots. Rylan had begun to argue that time was far more important than mere wood when the roots abruptly began to widen around the path, and it stretched ahead of them, strewn with leaves like a golden carpet.

The roots crawled along the edge of the expanse and then speared up, creating a border than resembled a railing. Branches dipped from the trees around the path and then arched up and over. Enlin could not think how it was possible that nature itself had decided to behave in such a way.

Rylan expressed his unrest verbally at the change, his hand resting on the hilt of his sword as it had whenever he had had a hand free from maneuvering through the difficult forest foliage.

Enlin simply led his horse forward, grateful for the ability to cover more ground, and watching for what might lead to a home. Did Alayna reside within the trees to shield herself from others, or to shield others from her?

"Don't believe I've ever heard anyone mention this forest in anything but unfavorable terms. I doubt many made it past the tangle to see this!" Weston too kept his eye roving for possible veering trails that could lead to their objective. There were breaks in the roots, but none so far had seemed to have a purpose.

The colors were brilliant and so vibrant they appeared to pulse light into the air. Enlin bent and picked up a couple of the leaves scattered over the dirt, rubbing them between his fingers. They felt like silk. A breeze lifted the hair resting on his shoulders and leaves scurried up into the air, joining the breeze.

Frowning when the flutter gathered and was blown into a wide trunk ahead of them, Enlin watched the leaves fall as the breeze died. He made his way toward it and saw when he was almost upon it that another path veered to the right, all but hidden by several smaller trees clumped together. There was not enough room for a horse.

"Rylan, this is the way we go."

Rylan stopped beside him, shaking his head. "I don't think this is a good idea at all. We can't just leave the horses here."

Weston was already tying his reins to a low branch. "The horses will be fine, Rylan. Let us make haste. The supper hour is upon us!"

"You assume we will find someone willing to feed us," Rylan grumbled, and drew his sword as he motioned for Prince Enlin to follow Weston. Rylan took up the rear, his fingers tight around the hilt of his weapon. He needed to remember to stop allowing the Prince to persuade him against following protocol. Having a few extra men would have done much to ease some of his anxiety.

The pathway was narrow and twisted, making it impossible to see ahead. The leaves were all gold, and the light had a blue tint. The air was warmer. Behind him, Rylan's breathing was heavy and Enlin glanced back. It was obvious that Rylan was unsettled. His eyes darted over everything, his sword was ready in his hand, and his knees were loose to spring into action if needed.

Shaking his head, Enlin chuckled softly. He was not afraid. His instincts were telling him that they were being welcomed. If the breeze had not lifted the leaves and drawn his eye, they would have missed the path they were currently on.

It was not long before Weston motioned for the Prince to come alongside him in the narrow space. "What do you see, Prince?"

The trail where Weston stood had widened and forked off in a couple of directions. Thick tree trunks larger than any he had ever seen were ahead of them, with many roots from the surrounding trees snaking up, out, and around many of them. Forward would be impossible.

Weston lifted a hand, pointing with two fingers. Enlin

followed the direction and saw what Weston had patiently waited for him to see. A thin tendril of smoke.

"Somewhere in this tangle of tree limbs is a home." Weston moved to the nearest of the larger trunks and began to examine the crevices and shadows.

"Or a trap," Rylan added wryly, positioning himself as guard in front of Prince Enlin.

"My lady!" Weston called out. "We wish to speak with you!"

Rylan protested, spreading his arms out as much as he could and planting his feet, hovering in front of his Prince as best he could to guard him from any possible attack.

"You needn't prepare for a battle where there will be none," a soft voice said.

Rylan shifted his body weight toward the speaker.

Enlin watched a woman glide through the slim opening in the trees to their left, her hair as golden as the leaves and her eyes as blue as a cloudless sky. His father's description had been accurate.

Her eyes were on him, steady and heavy with emotion. "Come inside, Prince, and I will tell you what you seek."

"I'm hoping you'll be serving scones with that," Weston said amicably as he pushed past Rylan to smile at the woman and bow. "My lady, it is a pleasure to find you!"

"You may have a different opinion after we speak," the lady cautioned as she turned to lead the way.

Enlin shook his head as Rylan hissed out an argument against following. "I need to hear what it is that she has to say."

Huffing out his frustration, Rylan followed because Enlin gave him no choice.

CHAPTER 11

a raised root coming out of a side of the huge hollow tree they entered provided seating in front of a crudely built table already set for tea. Rylan did not sit. The woman ignored him as she poured for Enlin and Weston and retrieved a plate of biscuits. Weston thanked her and graciously waited until she sat and indicated for him to help himself before taking one from the tray.

Enlin's quick glance around the space did not reveal much. Part of the area was curtained off. The rest held a chair next to a small table, a kitchenette, some cupboards, and the table at which they sat. Nothing adorned the walls, and he saw no trinkets or material possessions scattered around.

She waited for him to finish his appraisal, her eyes on him, her hands in her lap. "Do you know why I have come?" he questioned.

"You are betrothed."

"How could you know that?" Rylan demanded.

She did not look away from the Prince. "The town speaks. I knew that you would come."

"Have the things that you foretold to me on that night changed?"

She gave a slight shake of her head. "I am sorry, Prince Enlin, but no. If you marry, your Kingdom will fall."

"Well," Weston declared. He lifted his mug. "This brew is tasty. Your words are unfortunate." He leaned back against the wall near his shoulder, tapping his fingers on the table as he regarded the woman. "There is nothing that can be done to change this?"

Blue eyes shifted from the Prince to Weston. "Your heart is loyal, but soon you will be asked to betray your Prince."

Frowning, Weston straightened and leaned forward. "I would never betray Prince Enlin!" For the first time, unrest curled in Weston's belly and a shiver skittered over his skin. He had not believed the hushed, frightened tales of her, but now looking into her depthless eyes, he could understand the fear that had overtaken those he had spoken to.

She was not like other people. There was something about her that set her apart.

Again, her gaze shifted, back to Enlin. "Why do you marry her?"

"She will be ruined if I do not."

"And yet, you know the consequences if you do."

Enlin pushed his tea aside and leaned into the space between him. "Tell me how you could know such a thing, Alayna. My father has told me of your affair. Theara has told me that my mother despised you. She also told me I was not meant to be born, and yet, my mother went on to birth two more children. Perhaps this is a ploy for revenge?"

"Prince Enlin..." Sorrow clouded her eyes. "Your sisters were not sired by the King."

"This is treason!" Rylan exclaimed, anger propelling him to stand over her with a glower.

Enlin held up a hand to silence him. "You cannot tell me

such a thing without telling me everything. How could you know they are not the Kings children?"

She reached out to take one of his hands. Her fingers were warm and as soft as the leaf he had held. A storm full of tears filled her eyes. "Your birth... your mother attempted to... terminate you. We managed to save you, but there would have been no way for her to carry another baby to term."

Reeling, Enlin pulled is hand free and stood. There was nowhere to go in the small space. He looked at Rylan, trying to gather his emotions, needing the opposing voice to speak now and tell her that she was wrong. Instead, the look on Rylan's face pushed the knife deeper. "You knew?" he breathed.

Rylan shook his head. "I didn't believe that it was true. I thought it was exaggeration and rumor. Your mother was not liked, Prince Enlin. I just thought... I..." Rylan closed his eyes, pressing his lips together.

"It is not until now that things begin to make sense. Little pieces, things that were said..."

"Is nothing as it seems?" Enlin demanded, facing Alayna. "Does the King know?" Did his sisters? And if the King was not their father, then who was? This would crush both of his sisters. Perhaps even destroy their lives if the truth became known.

"I cannot tell you if the King is aware."

"What other pieces of my life have you to tear to shreds? Are you a sorceress then, after all?" His feet were heavy as he made his way back to the table and sat. He would hear it all. He had not come this far to shy away from whatever other truths she had to share.

"I am not a sorceress!" Alayna stood with a swish of her skirts at his words, anger making her eyes flash with light. "I tire of this lie! You will call it what you wish, but my spirit speaks to me of things. How can I not share when I know that if the listener heeds the words that I speak much sorrow will be avoided?"

He watched her set the kettle back on to heat. The tea had grown cold. Enlin felt much the same. He had not been prepared. He had thought, and hoped, that she would ease his burden by telling him her words had not been truth. His expectations had been unrealistic.

Her hand trembled slightly, the tell a gentle rattle of the teapot as she put it on its burner. The label bothered her.

"Theara spoke of a threat," Enlin continued. "She said that you were meant to protect my mother. Was there a conspiracy for her life?"

"No, Prince." Alayna gathered the mugs and emptied them, before bringing them back. "I was there only to protect you. I came as soon as I knew the Queen was with child."

Alayna scooped out dried tea leaves and added them to a small mesh bag. The stems were plentiful in the forest. She had found them in no other. Once, she had thought to sell them in the town, but the people had mocked her for her potions.

"I feared that she would find some way to harm you, but she valued her life and was cautious about her attempts to preserve herself." Setting the bag inside of the pot to steep, Alayna carried it to the table.

Weston watched her as warily as the others but did push his mug forward.

"Your mother was desperate by the time you were almost to term," Alayna continued as she poured. "So desperate that she tried to... abort you. She knew that once she went into labor she would be surrounded by women, and she would have no other chance."

"That is horrible!" Rylan accepted the mug that was held out, disgust clear on his features. "I don't care to know how a woman would even attempt such a thing."

Enlin had no interest in knowing either. "And what of my

69

destiny? Theara spoke of that as well. Why was I so important? Was it only because of my gender?"

Alayna nodded. "Yes. I knew that you were the only male your father would sire." She sighed heavily, cradling her mug, and staring down into the blonde liquid. Her words softened to barely above a whisper. "Once, I thought that perhaps I could redeem myself by doing what I could to save your Kingdom. But I failed."

Enlin watched a tear fall into the tea in her hands.

"I can no longer hear the song even in the quietest moments. If it is silent for me..."

"What song do you speak of?" Enlin asked, no longer sure if she spoke to them.

Her lashes flickered and she gave a quick shake of her head. "It matters not, Prince Enlin," she said firmly and stood, her chin lifting as she regarded him. "You have made your choice. There is nothing I can do to help you."

"So that's it, then?" Weston asked. "You have nothing more to offer the man who will one day be your King? He could appeal your banishment!"

"I am afraid what I have seen will come to pass. Your Prince sought the truth, and that is the truth. My banishment matters not. I am at home here. I cannot regain what I have lost."

"Dare I inquire if you have made the forest what it is, or if the forest was this way before you inhabited it?" Rylan spoke with no animosity. He was merely curious.

Blue eyes still glistening with unshed tears met Rylans for only a moment. "I cannot remember."

CHAPTER 12

*H*er last words niggled at Enlin. Was it a coincidence that she had chosen those words? It had struck him as they'd reached their horses that Alayna bore a slight resemblance to Breeon. Only in the coloring of the hair and skin, but it was enough to make him ponder.

Rylan and Weston were quiet and Enlin was glad to have his thoughts uninterrupted. He had much to process. His quest had reaped no solution.

Where the path narrowed, Enlin swung down off his horse and loosened his furs. "We will camp here for the night."

With no argument, they each claimed a spot and carefully built a fire. Alayna had given Rylan bread and cheese. She had refused payment, but Enlin had instructed Rylan to leave a small bag of gold outside of the door knowing she would find it after they were gone.

Weston was the first to speak as they each settled with a portion of the meal. "I cannot imagine how you are handling everything we have just heard, Prince. Your burden is far greater than I ever considered."

"You cannot marry Lady Breeon," Rylan stated.

"So, he saves the Kingdom, but ruins the lady?" Weston questioned with a wave of his bread. "Your knowledge of our Prince is astoundingly incorrect for one who is so close. He will find another way."

Enlin shook his head. "There is no other way. I must choose. Let the Kingdom fall, or ruin Breeon."

"Or she could die," Rylan said.

Startled, Enlin reared back. "You cannot be serious!" Mind whirling, Enlin stood, wrapping his hand around the smooth metal hilt of the sword at his side. "You speak of death as though it were a common solution! Have you secrets you have been hiding as well?"

Rylan set his food aside and ran a hand through his hair. "Prince, no! I meant only that we could arrange the appearance of her death, not cause it! It would free her from ruin and save the Kingdom!"

Weston blew out a long breath and reached out to clap Rylan's shoulder. "My friend, for a moment I feared betrayal." He motioned to Enlin's fur. "Prince, let us relax. Rylan has a valid alternative here and we should examine it. It could work."

"Yes," Rylan agreed. "She could become ill. It would not be that far-fetched considering the way she came to you. We could arrange to have her taken to a Kingdom where she would be unknown."

"Or she could reside with the sorceress," Weston suggested.

Enlin frowned. He didn't care for either option. Both meant he would never see Breeon again. Glancing back down the path, he reconsidered. The Woods of Valoria were not far from his Kingdom. Perhaps it was a good idea. Alayna was alone and likely had been for years. And, if the appearance of her humble home gave credence to his belief that she had little, he could send Breeon with provisions to make them both comfortable.

"Absolutely not," Rylan countered. "It is far too close. The likelihood of someone discovering the truth would be too high. We cannot take that chance."

Enlin clenched his teeth and held his tongue. Rylan was right. Valoria Woods was off the table. "Who would we trust to be involved and to get her out of the Kingdom? I keep my circle close."

Weston added more wood to the fire. "Should I be disturbed that both of you seem to be having a hard time with that question? The Kingdom is at peace. I'm afraid this adventure has altered my view of the way things are. Or seem to be." Scowling, Weston poked at the burning coals. "Were. Goodness, my perspective has been destroyed."

He had his wife to think of. If the ominous premonitions were a real possibility, he had to consider how best to care for her safety. He refused to think of what she had told him he would be asked to do. She was wrong. He would never betray his future King.

"I'm sorry, Weston," Enlin apologized. He had not meant to bring shadows into anyone's life.

"What will you tell the King?" Rylan queried.

"I think it best to say nothing to the King." Enlin did not want to know how much of what he had just learned had already been known to his father. He hadn't even settled his mind about his father's indiscretions as of yet.

"We need to settle on a plan of action before we arrive back in the Kingdom. Our players will need to be gathered and things set in motion soon. We don't have much time."

"I have not yet agreed, Rylan," Enlin shot out. He didn't like that Rylan's offering seemed to be the only feasible solution. Sending Breeon off where he could not protect her made him unhappy. There would be no guarantees the outcome would be as they intended.

"Unless, of course, you feel marrying her outweighs the

risk of your Kingdom?" Weston inquired. He tucked his tongue in his cheek to keep a smile from escaping.

Tensing, Enlin met Weston's eyes and saw the mirth there. He was not being challenged.

A smile broke over his friend's face. Weston could tell Enlin had no idea there was far more than his feelings for his Kingdom at play. "We could fight, Prince Enlin," Weston continued. "Whatever happens, if the woman is worth it to you, we will fight."

"Fight?" Rylan unsheathed the knife at his side and ran his finger over the blade. "The Kingdom has fought no battles in years."

"If we're going to talk about fake murder plots, we should also discuss what exactly the sorceress means by 'the Kingdom will fall.'" Weston arched a brow at Rylan. The man was annoyingly cynical. If they were to be spending more time together, he was going to have to find a way to help the man relax.

Enlin knew Weston was right. He had not given time to dissecting the words as was being suggested.

At his nod, Weston continued. "Perhaps the woman is... already betrothed. An angry suitor could arrive at the castle gates with an army intent on taking back his bride."

"You're being ridiculous," Rylan scoffed.

"No, he's not," Enlin reprimanded. "She has no memory. It is possible she is already spoken for."

Rylan stabbed his knife into the ground. "More likely is the plot we have already considered. If she is a pawn in a conspiracy, the wedding could be the catalyst for an uprising."

Weston pulled his own knife free and began to polish it. "Rylan has a point. I was unaware that your betrothed suffers from memory loss?"

Resigned, Enlin explained the circumstances that had led

to where they were. He trusted Weston and knew none of it would be shared, not even with his wife.

"Interesting," Weston said when Enlin finished. "What do your instincts tell you, Prince?"

"That she does not plot against me," Enlin answered without hesitation.

A corner of Weston's mouth quirked. "Because you are sure, or because you want it to be the truth?"

"It is the truth," Enlin countered flatly.

Weston laughed, falling back on his fur, one hand pressing against his belly as the laugh continued.

Enlin did not care for the response or understand what had struck Weston so comically. He took his glare off Weston to arch a brow at Rylan, annoyed when he saw that Rylan was doing his best to hide his own smile.

"What could possibly be so amusing about what I said?"

Rolling back up, Weston did his best to contain his mirth. "Forgive, me Prince, but I had not realized how taken you are with your future bride!"

"One, I am not, and two, I still fail to see the humor."

Clearing his throat, Weston tugged off a boot and dropped it to the ground. "One, you are taken with her. And two, I laugh because it puts me in good cheer to know your heart has finally been claimed. I feared you would spend the rest of your days alone. I, being the happily married man I am, would not wish such a fate upon my future King." The second boot landed beside the first and Weston separated his furs and slid between the folds.

Enlin said nothing, only stared at the man while the words repeated in his head. Had Weston latched onto something he had missed?

A good King questioned everything. He had been taught that. And while the recent bout of secrets that had come to light suggested he had not learned that lesson well, it was one he intended to pay far more attention to.

Enlin looked across the fire at Rylan. "Have you your own thoughts to add? Do you believe him to be right?"

"I believe you must come to your own conclusion about Lady Breeon, Prince."

"So, we fight," Weston concluded, manipulating the cloth beneath his head into a pillow.

"It is possible nothing will happen," Rylan said. "We have strong allies. If anyone threatens the peace of the Kingdom, we will have a full army at our disposal."

Enlin thought of Breeon's pronouncement after she had first met his father. He had not shared that information. Breeon's words strengthened Alayna's own prediction.

Could there be more than one meaning? He needed to question Breeon further about what exactly she had seen and felt. Could it simply be that his marriage would change the Kingdom as they knew it? No Queen had reigned by the King's side in more than two decades.

"You have much to consider, Prince. I will take first watch. We will talk more thoroughly in the morning when you decide how we will proceed. Get some rest."

Enlin appreciated that Rylan was allowing him time to sift through his thoughts. He doubted sleep would come but he made up his own pallet and stretched out to try.

CHAPTER 13

$\mathcal{T}$he market on the castle grounds was bustling when they passed with their horses on the way to the stables. Many called out greetings and congratulated the Prince on the upcoming nuptials.

Weston had returned home. Enlin had given neither of the men a decision. If he chose to go forward with the marriage, there was still the problem of Breeon's own proclamation that she could not marry to be dealt with. Nor would he fake her death if she was opposed to it. He had concluded that first he must speak with her before he allowed his mind to rest on anything concrete.

Unsure where he would find her, Enlin made his way toward the rooms where his sisters resided. He wanted to see them, if only to look upon their faces and determine if he saw any resemblance to someone other than his father.

He found Nyala first, alone with a basket of what looked like weeds at her side in the sitting area that separated her suite from her sisters. She smiled at him as he bent to kiss her cheek.

"Nya, I have missed you." Her hair was a mass of curls as usual. Enlin picked a twig out of it. "Have you been wandering the gardens again?" Nya had always loved being outside and in the summer could often be found in the flower beds, despite the protests of her governess.

"There are no flowers for your wedding, En. I thought I could make something beautiful for Breeon to wear in her hair."

Enlin sat on an empty space on the settee and picked a stalk out of the basket. "Have you spoken to her?"

A spattering of freckles was visible on each of Nya's cheeks. Enlin had no freckles. Their hair coloring was similar, her skin tone paler than his, and her eyes were blue. Kahlee had dark hair as well and her eyes were brown. Did Kahlee and Nya share the same father? And if his mother had not birthed his sisters, who had?

"She has spoken to me," Nya answered quietly, weaving strands of the weeds together in her hands. Her fingers paused. "I like her very much." Blue eyes peered up at him from beneath dark lashes.

Enlin had not given any thought to eye color before the question of parentage had been raised, but now he was struck by how different one pair of blue eyes could be from another. While Alayna's had been clear and light, his sisters were dark like the waters of the lake that sat on the western edge of the Kingdom.

"She is more than I ever expected for you."

Unsure how to answer such a statement, Enlin did not.

"I thought perhaps you meant to be alone for your whole life,"

Nya said softly as she went back to twining the stems together. Enlin watched as a circle began to take shape.

If a battle was to be fought, he would need to consider the safety of his family. Blood or not, he had known them as nothing else. He wondered how his mother had managed to pretend she carried a child for nine months without his father learning the truth.

Frowning, Enlin pushed the thought away. "What do you think of her lack of memory, Nya?"

She had called him En for as long as he could remember. As a toddler beginning to speak, he had teasingly called her Nya back and her delighted giggle had been all that was needed to continue the exchange of nicknames, which were not commonly used within the Kingdoms.

He had never managed to form any such bond with Kahlee. She was as indifferent and spoiled as Nya was shy and withdrawn.

"Her heart is genuine. I would be happy to call her a sister." Nya lifted the thin wreath that had taken shape. "It really needs some color. Her hair would be so pretty adorned with flowers, don't you think?"

Enlin thought of the brightly colored leaves within the Woods of Valoria. Had there been flowers that he had not seen?

He reached out to brush his thumb over his sister's cheek. "I think you should know that I love you, Nyala, and that I will do whatever it takes to keep you safe and happy."

The wreath settled in her lap. Her eyes held his. He was the only one he had ever seen her fully look at. Everyone else she avoided eye contact with.

"I do not fear that you will change because you will marry. I know that you love me."

He would let her think his upcoming marriage was why he had spoken the words. "Have you seen Breeon today?"

"At breakfast. She sat with me."

"And after?"

"She is in her rooms. She is being properly outfitted, per the King's orders."

Which meant she would have an entourage.

"She does not like the swooning of her Ladies-in-waiting. I believe she called them 'swans.'" Nya giggled and picked through the basket at her side.

"I don't suppose it would be proper for me to intrude?"

"I would think not." Nya reached up and patted his cheek. "She is very beautiful. Inside and out. It is like the light is in her eyes. While in her presence, I thought more than once that I heard a song in the air."

"A song?" Alayna had spoken of a song, Enlin remembered. "I'm not sure what you mean?"

Nya lifted a shoulder. Enlin grinned. Her governess would scold her for the gesture. Ladies did not shrug.

Her fingers trailed gently over a delicate juniper cutting she had worked into the wreath. "I am not sure either," she whispered, her eyes downcast. "I thought perhaps I was imagining it, but..."

"Go on," Enlin encouraged. Nya feared being ridiculed, even by him, though he had never done so.

"I concentrated to be sure, and I heard it again and again. It was so beautiful and entrancing."

Her lashes fluttered up and her head lifted slightly so she peered up at him from beneath them. "The song was there, soft like the whisper of the air that ruffles the stems of the flowers in the spring."

She began to hum, her fingers absently tracing the lines of a dusty miller leaf.

Enlin thought the harmony familiar. When had he heard it? He was sure it had not been recently.

"Do you ever feel that we are not alone in this world, En?"

The remnants of the song fled at her words. "What do you mean, Nya?"

Again, she would not look at him. He knew her well enough to know she feared what he would think of her next words.

"There are times when I feel the presence of... someone, so strongly that it is not possible to deny the existence of it."

The words brought Enlin no comfort. Rather, with the threat of unrest at his heels, they brought a frisson of fear. He reached out to clasp one of Nya's small hands. "Is it possible that you are being followed?"

He watched an answering fear widen her eyes and she pulled back away from him. "Followed? Why would you think that? I meant only that I feel a presence, but not... not around me."

Flustered, Nya's words tumbled over each other. "I explain things so poorly. I apologize, En. I should not have spoken so outrageously."

"Nya, I need you to assure me you do not believe you are being followed. I cannot rest easy if I think it is possible."

"No one follows me, En." A sad smile lifted just the corners of her lips. "Does anyone but you really know that I even exist?"

"Nya..."

She busied her hands in the basket, picking out long stems. "You needn't placate me, En. I know the truth."

Enlin took the stems from her and returned them to the basket, setting it aside. Shifting, he gathered his sister close against his side, wishing there was something he could do to ease the burden of identity she had taken on as who she was.

"Some people only see what is just beyond the eye and not into the heart. Someday, you will be seen for all that you are."

Nya dipped her head into the crook just beneath his arm. The words sank deep, and she cradled them as she tried to believe they were true. She would not tell him she wasn't brave enough to accept the words.

"Perhaps you would consider drawing Breeon away so that I could speak with her? They would not frown upon your presence, would they?"

Nya was glad that Enlin had shifted the subject but did not like what he suggested. She caught her lower lip between her teeth. "Must I?"

The words where whispered, a sure sign that he had

pushed too far. Enlin ran his hand over the softness of Nya's hair, wondering if things would have been different for her had she had the love of a mother to raise her.

He could well imagine the chaos of dressmakers and noble ladies gathered around piles fabrics and discussing fashion. The last place his shy sister would want to be.

"No," he soothed. "I will speak with her later." Rising, Enlin made a decision to seek out his father. He could not avoid the man forever and there were things that needed to be said.

CHAPTER 14

*T*he King was in his private chambers, and it was clear that he was distressed. He paced, his face taut, his hands clasped behind his back. "Where have you been?" he demanded as Enlin entered.

"I had business to attend to," Enlin answered shortly.

"You should be taking carriage rides and strolls through the market with your betrothed," the King reprimanded.

"There is time enough for that." A carriage ride would be the perfect place to discuss things privately with Breeon. He doubted there would be time for one before supper. His recollections of Kahlee's dressmaking sessions were of long days that resulted in preening prances throughout the dining hall for weeks.

The pacing abruptly halted. His father's expression was harsh when he turned to face his son. "I have decided to summon our Knights."

Kingdom Silvera had long operated with its own set of rules. They were the central Kingdom between mountains to the north and south, with several small towns scattered beyond the castle walls.

The closest surrounding Kingdoms: Vilitia, Vyell, Aviore

and Ovsia were allies and each had a company of Knights kept trained and ready, despite the lack of conflict in the past.

Enlin was startled but stayed still and quiet for a moment. If a battle was to be fought, this was exactly what needed to happen. Why his father had determined it was needed was puzzling. "For what reason?"

"I fear a plot. I have wrestled with this. A call to arms could signal there is unrest, but a marriage is a good enough reason to claim a need for extra men." The King crossed his arms, his eyes on the woven rug beneath his feet.

"I have sent messengers to quietly gather the army. I have asked that they arrive before the wedding, without fanfare."

"Is there something you aren't telling me, Father?" There were shadows in his father's eyes when he raised them and Enlin could some of the darkness beginning to gather in the hollows beneath as well.

The King spun and made his way to one of the tall windows that looked out over the land. "My sins chase me. I have had the thought it would be easier to imprison your betrothed as a traitor, but it would make no difference."

A coldness gathered in Enlin's stomach. "Has something come to light since we spoke last?" Was Breeon in danger? If his father determined her to be a traitor, there would be nothing he could do to save her.

"The woman that spoke to you about your marriage..."

His father's back and shoulders were straight, the never-ending stance of a King claiming his position.

"She spoke things to me as well. I did not listen."

Enlin opened his mouth to tell the King he already knew but the King had begun to speak again, so he waited.

"At first, I believed it all to be just stories. An amusement for her to spin her tales. Her eyes, Enlin... I would forget she was speaking while I gazed upon her beauty. Her voice was

84

like a song. The words became nothing more than a melody and so I was content to let them flow without substance."

The poetic words were odd coming from his father. It was not a nostalgic reminiscence. His tone was too somber for that. There again, was another reference to a song. To yet another secret.

The King clasped his hands behind his back. "How could one believe such things anyway? Angel wings and songs that rise to the heavens to touch the heart of God Himself. And creatures unlike us who choose to be. Wars and supernatural battles fought and won in impossible ways. All of it was far too implausible to believe."

Enlin was beginning to think there was no point to what his father was sharing. He wanted to question the King about his mother's death. Theara had said it was no accident. If his father knew the truth of his sisters, would he also know of his mothers' true demise?

And if the King did not know, what would it mean if he did for

Nyala? For Kahlee?

Should he ask his questions while the King was lost in his reflections of the past? Would he get another chance?

"She warned me, Enlin. All those years ago, she warned me. And I did not listen. And I am afraid somehow, this woman you have brought here to take as your bride, was sent by her. To warn me again. Only this time, it is too late."

Slowly, the King turned, his face grave. "I am afraid, Enlin, my wedding gift to you will be war."

CHAPTER 15

"*Y*ou aren't making any sense."

Alayna could not have sent Breeon. She would have said.

The Woods of Valoria and his cabin were close in proximity.

Could it be possible? Enlin shook his head in denial. He had given her every opportunity to tell him everything.

"She did not send her," Enlin said aloud, but the words were not convincing even to him. How ironic it would be had they chosen to place Breeon with Alayna? His need to speak with Breeon almost made him turn to seek her, propriety be ignored.

The King began to walk toward him. "Enlin, she told me about the feather from an angel wing would signal the end of peace for my Kingdom. That beneath the feet of my enemy, the feathers would be trampled. Take care, she said. 'Take care to hold what is precious close, because when the last iridescent feather fades into dust, the song will end and there will be peace no more.'"

Songs again. Enlin was struggling to keep up. To gather all the secrets and stories and truths together and hold onto what mattered. To what was true. Was this how Breeon felt, grasping at slivers to put together a picture of what you could not see?

"My men brought me one, Enlin."

The fire snapped, an ember sparking out from the stones to fizzle to its death on the stone floor.

He stared at the man before him. One who had never voiced a weakness in his presence before. Now, he was placing the words of a woman as the catalyst for the death of the life they knew.

"A feather, Enlin. A thing of fantasy when she spoke of it. Not reality. And yet, it is unlike anything I have ever seen before. It is there, but it is not there. It glitters like the first dusting of snow as it begins to stick. Like diamonds. And what am I do, Enlin, except call forth the armies and watch the stones of this castle crumble as your bride foresaw? As a woman from my past warned while I turned a deaf ear and thought her fanciful."

The heat from the fire was too hot. The light too bright.

"I try to recall if there were clues, offered to me as a way to stop it all, but I only hear her speaking of that which is precious being taken from me. I would think she means you, Enlin. You are the future of this Kingdom. Without you, it is lost."

Could Alayna have sent her? Was there perhaps some plot after all? An attempt at revenge for acts his father had committed against her? He was questioning every moment and every word as he spun to walk away from the vision of the death of his Kingdom.

He needed to find the woman he was meant to take as his wife. Would speaking the name of the sorceress bring back her memory? Had Alayna cast some spell so Breeon would remember only what it was she had wanted her to speak?

What if it was another warning? He had been about to choose not to listen. Enlin had decided he would marry her and if he was honest with himself, he had made the decision before the sorceress had confirmed her words.

There were too many hallways. The Lions roared at him from the tapestries on the walls. His boots thudded on the stone.

Enlin did not knock. Nor did he have the startled servant announce him. He scanned the clusters of women for Breeon and did not see the widening eyes or the sudden whispers as heads leaned in close together.

Breeon sat amidst it all, her beauty mesmerizing. She was swathed in gold, the layers of it spreading as she rose at his appearance. The sleeves of the gown were sheer and flowed over her arms to balloon slightly over the gathering at her wrists.

Cream-colored embroidered flowers swirled over the soft fabric and made him think of the sunny days of the coming spring, not the cold of the winter seeping into his soul.

The women parted for her. He was not so lost in turmoil that he did not recognize another woman would have apologized for his intrusion and docilely inquired as to his needs. Breeon did not. She moved gracefully through the chaos of the room to stop for only a moment in front of him before taking his hand and leading him from the room, another faux pas that she cared nothing about.

Clinging to his senses, Enlin tightened his hold on her fingers and turned her first down one hallway, and then another, to a set of stairs set behind a wall, down into an empty room that had not been used in centuries. He pushed the heavy door closed and secured the thick wood slab into the metal arms that would keep anyone from entering.

The room was cold, and it occurred to him as he turned away from the door that taking her to a dark cold room alone had probably not been the best idea. Finding the torch set on the wall to one side, Enlin lit it after fumbling around for the supplies he knew were below it in a bowl on a pedestal.

"I do not want you to be a traitor," he said to her when he faced her.

Could they have been happy? If things were different and she became his bride, could they have defied the odds of aristocracy and found what Weston and his wife had?

"I am not a traitor."

"My Kingdom is falling, just as you said."

The gold danced in her eyes from the firelight reflected off the torch. "It is because of me?"

"Do you know a woman named Alayna? Or of the Woods of Valoria?"

He watched her contemplate his words. Saw the discouragement and frustration wash over her face before she shook her head gently. "No, I do not believe I do."

"I no longer know how to proceed with any of this. Rylan suggests we fake your death and Weston says we should fight. I had determined to fight, but now..."

"Where would I go, Prince Enlin?" She walked toward him, closing the short distance. Her chin lifted as she looked up at him and brought her hand up to rest on his chest. "Have you found out something about me?"

"No. I have only discovered that it is true I should not marry you, and whether I do or not, it seems my Kingdom is doomed."

Enlin's breath caught as the words he had just spoken flared. "Whether I marry you or not, Breeon. My Kingdom will fall either way." Beneath her hand, his heart began to beat faster.

The gold in her eyes held his attention and he found he had to think about keeping his breaths even. She was far too close. And not close enough. "I can marry you," he said, tearing his gaze from hers to look at her mouth.

She could be his wife. Did he want a wife? She would be

his to protect. He would no longer be alone. Did he want that? There would be someone to share his struggles with, his triumphs, the simplicity of his days and the tribulations of ruling a Kingdom. If he had one. There would be no need to seek the solitude of his cabin to quiet the rumblings of his thoughts. He would have her to turn to. If he chose.

Breeon stepped back, her hand falling to her side. "I cannot marry you."

For a moment, his breath caught in his lungs, and he had to focus to free it again to breathe. He curled his fingers at his side to stop himself for reaching out for her closeness again. "But you cannot tell me why."

The cold had consumed him. The fate set out for him, and his Kingdom had begun with him, falling at his feet into dust.

"I do not think I want to leave," she said slowly. "But neither do I think I have a choice. Faking one's death seems very wrong, but I am unsure what other options I have?"

You could stay, Enlin thought.

"We had few to begin with," he said instead. Enlin had again and again cycled through every option he could think of, except the one that Breeon had chosen. He had spent his sleepless nights examining every possibility that could befall the Kingdom if war came.

He had listed reasons why she could not marry him, but he had never considered that she herself would refuse, despite her statements that she could not. She had little choice in the matter.

And yet, she was choosing the option he had least expected. The one had had not bothered to come up with options for getting her out. It was a hard truth to look at the woman in front of him and admit even in the small amount of time she had been in his life; he had decided he wanted her to stay there.

That didn't make sense, either. Why, after all the years he had chosen to be alone did he choose the one woman he could have no future with? Enlin had learned self-control; taught himself to put his emotions away and deny any attractions that may have come his way. Now, he wondered if perhaps there had never been any attractions at all, and it had been easy for him to believe he had achieved his goal only because it had not been difficult.

Grasping at what resolve he could find, Enlin clenched his jaw and determined there was no choice. She had just taken it from him. He would bury whatever he was feeling and simply convince himself she was no different than any other woman he had met.

Turning, he unlatched the door and opened it. "We will speak again when I have come up with a plan. There are few I choose to trust with such a thing, and there is a possibility this plot could fail, and it will end in your death."

His hand curled around the thick wood of the door as he moved aside to let her pass. When she was in the hall, Enlin extinguished the torch and closed the door behind him.

"If I did marry you, Prince Enlin, it could result in both of our deaths," Breeon said quietly into the dark hall.

Thinking of his father's words, Enlin tried not to think that perhaps fate had already chosen for all of them, and Breeon was right.

CHAPTER 16

*W*ith Breeon's decision in mind, finalizing a plan had become priority. He had spent a restless night thinking of little else. After breakfast, he had intended to continue making plans, but Telphee had called him into a meeting with the King and a few other advisors. Enlin had been unfocused and ran through scenarios in his head while Telphee's voice had droned.

Now, free, Enlin ordered a servant to see that he and Rylan's horses were prepared and sought out his friend.

There was a hint of warmth in the air as they galloped across the open fields, signaling spring was making its debut of the season.

To obtain privacy, they sought the waters of the Illuvian, the western lake he had likened Nyala's eyes to. They rode hard and allowed the horses more leisure as they drew close so they could talk.

"We have limited time, Enlin. Wedding preparations mean the castle is at high capacity and more people watching will make things more difficult."

"You are right. She has chosen, Rylan. We will need to be

mindful that every step is well executed and that it happens quickly."

"Have you a plan then, Prince?"

"Not one I like. It puts others in danger." "And the alternative?"

If there was one, Enlin had not thought of it, but it made nothing easier. "I could think of only a handful that I feel we can trust completely. I have chosen Theara, but I haven't spoken to her as of yet."

It had not been an easy choice. There was her family to think of, and if she was caught, it could mean death for all of them. Or life, if removing Breeon from the equation had the desired effect. His father's dilemma would have to be dealt with separately.

Theara seemed to be the most viable option. She already knew of his secret and there was a personal connection. To him, to his family, and to the Kingdom as a whole. She would want peace to continue as much as anyone, and from the words she had spoken during their past meeting, he had wondered if she had been a part of the scheme that had ended his mother's life.

If Rylan agreed with his choice, he would seek Theara's presence and question her further. He wanted no more facts to defy the reality that he had known before Breeon had arrived at his door.

It was then everything had changed, and while she seemed to be at the center of it, he could not convince himself she was the cause. So, facts he would gather, whether he wanted to know them or not.

Enlin had filled Rylan in on the mysteries falling around them like dominoes, including the things his father had told him. Whatever happened, he needed someone who knew all the aspects at play in case he himself became incapacitated and could not move forward with the plan, when they came up with one.

"I think she is a good choice," Rylan commented. "She was invested in your birth enough to keep her secret all these years. We could also ask Alayna for help."

"I still fear her involvement in some way that has not yet come to light." Enlin had been unable to put an end to the suspicion that Alayna knew more about Breeon than she had said. Who his bride was had not come up, but if Alayna had heard any of the gossip that had spread so quickly, it was possible that she had known.

He could think of no good reason for her not to share any information she might have had that would help the cause for the Kingdom. Whatever happened, Enlin was sure that he would see Alayna again.

"Breeon's death must be believable. It's too convenient to have her die in her sleep and be carried out in the morning."

The lake was before them. There were still pockets of ice that he could see. They glimmered in the light, adding to the mystical appearance of the lake as a whole.

Like the Woods of Valoria, Illuvian Lake was mysterious and often avoided. At times, it looked no different than any other lake, but then the light would shift and if you looked closely, you would see the soft flicker of transparent butterflies dancing in the air above the clear water or flitting about through the branches of the trees along the banks.

Enlin had spent many a day in his younger years sitting for hours watching for the sparkle of the wings. He had learned not to speak of the occurrences as many saw nothing at all after being near the water.

Dismounting, Enlin led his horse to the edge of a bank and allowed his horse to drink. He ran his hand over the neck of his stallion. "She could be thrown by a horse. That could be done with little audience."

Rylan stroked the neck of his own horse as it drank. "That could work. Her riding level is unknown. No one would think anything of the two of you going riding, with me as a chaperone. Do you trust that the Priest would declare her death?"

"No. But perhaps... when my mother died, who brought the news?"

Rylan shook his head. "I do not know. Telphee would."

"We cannot arouse Phee's suspicions in any way. We can ask him no questions." Thinking through the small list of those he felt he could trust again, Enlin thought again of Theara. And, how unsettling it was that after so many years of peace the list was so short.

"I will speak to Theara tonight and see if she is willing to assist us in our endeavor. She may well know the answer to our other questions as well."

"The sooner the better, Prince Enlin. Time is short."

Enlin frowned. He did not need the reminder. He well knew it was. He hated the secrets that had come to light within the past days, and now he was a part of creating more. He did not want to leave behind a legacy that was not pure and good. He had long admired what he had thought his father had accomplished and had made it a goal of his own to carry on what would someday become his to mold and shape.

"We will need someone to accompany Breeon to see that she is safe and can ensure that she can begin a life somewhere. It will need to be someone that will not raise any flags when they leave or do not return for some time." Enlin had no idea who to choose for that position and it concerned him that if he did not choose well, he might never know the outcome for Breeon.

The more thought he put into the plan, the less he liked it. How could he ensure her safety if he was not by her side to guarantee it? He verbalized the concern.

"Prince, you're going to have to leave some things to fate."

Enlin scowled at Rylan. "Have you ever considered there might be something more than fate?"

"I have no idea what you are talking about," Rylan answered.

Enlin wasn't sure himself. Perhaps he was just looking for something to calm the chaos his life had erupted into, but the last few days he had found himself searching for more. Many in the Kingdom spoke of gods, but he himself had thought it pointless to pray to objects or mythical figures that seemed to have more at stake for themselves than for the hearts of those seeking resolution from them.

"It would just be nice to have someone bigger than myself to reach out to for answers," he said in explanation.

Rylan looked at him steadily for a few moments. "I've never thought about it. Isn't that the job of the King, however?"

Once, Enlin would have agreed. "I'm struggling with my lack of adequate solutions for all of this and find the thought of divine help comforting at this moment. The King has his own concerns and offers little comfort for my own."

"Believing in such things is for fools," Rylan said, kicking at a loose stone.

Enlin wasn't so sure. He might have agreed even a week ago. Perhaps believing in a god made of wood or stone was for fools. But what if the Priest and his talk of a Creator who knew all and saw all was truth? He tried to recall some of the readings that droned on and on during the Sunday masses the family tolerated. Was he a fool to be questioning everything he had always chosen to ignore?

Something inside of him told him no. It was wise to look beyond all you knew to determine if one was missing something important. Something eternal, a voice whispered in his head.

Many a man had sought immortality and failed. Kingdoms had fallen for it. Blood had been spilled. Lives destroyed. For what? For lives full of questions trials and the pursuit of an impossible reality free from suffering?

One lived and strived to become the best version of themselves that they could be. Wasn't that all there was? And if some modicum of happiness could be found along the way for those in your care, one could die in peace knowing you had done all you could.

The choices he had made would have to be enough. A cloud shifted the light in the air and for a few moments, Enlin thought he saw the wings of the gossamer butterflies fluttering in the air, but when he squinted to be sure, he saw nothing. Enlin gathered his horse's reins and swung up onto the back of his horse. "I will question Theara. Perhaps it would be pertinent to question Weston as well. He may know of someone that we could trust."

Rylan mounted is horse. "Do not get discouraged, Prince. You and the King have loyal men on your side. We will do all we can to continue the legacy of peace that has been enjoyed by the Kingdom for so long."

Enlin appreciated the encouraging words, but his doubt grew, and his hope decreased. It was time to set his plan into motion. He did not want to wait much longer. It would help to settle his mind greatly to be able to place his focus elsewhere.

CHAPTER 17

"*P*rince Enlin."

Enlin had been unable to do anything to finalize any of his plans. Upon their return he had been summoned into a meeting of the Council as the Herald had announced the arrival of several Orders of Knights. For hours, their placement and dispersal had been discussed. It had been three days now and Enlin grew tired of the endless arguments and meticulous attention to strategy.

The King had fought no wars. He had not experienced ordering men into battle or faced the reality of the day-to-day care of an army. The older Knights who had fought for Enlin's grandfather had plenty of advice to offer, and many strong opinions on how to proceed.

Each of the Kingdoms allied with Silvera were structured so that if needed, half of each company of Knights could be sent to aid and still leave their Kingdoms well guarded.

Trained from boyhood, apprenticing as a Knight was an honorable position to be chosen for. It was common to see many a child sparring with wooden swords from young ages in the marketplace and in the training yards.

Children playing at war and preparing for one coming were two far different things.

"What is it, Telphee?" Telphee was the last person Enlin wanted to speak to. He was ready to break protocol and remove himself from any other planned meetings to seek out Theara.

Or Breeon. He had seen her fleetingly at supper each night, but he had not been seated by her side. Instead, he had watched her from his position near the King and had struggled to keep his mind focused on the trivialities of aristocratic complaints that were continuously brought before the King.

The growing numbers needing to be cared for had increased those seeking the King's presence as fear of the unknown spread throughout the Kingdom.

"Your presence is needed in your chamber, Your Highness." Telphee gave a slight bow and spread an arm to indicate the Prince should proceed him.

"For what?" Enlin tapped his heel on the stone beneath his boot.

"We have welcomed surrounding royals into our midst, and it is expected that you greet them accordingly. Your appearance should reflect the respect they deserve."

Barely managing the hold his tongue at the snide remark, as though he wasn't fully aware of etiquette, Enlin nodded and followed Telphee down the halls to his chamber. This was not the first greeting of royals. The Princes from Ovsia and Vilitia had both arrived the day before to offer their support.

Prince Gevin from Ovsia had married just over a year ago. Enlin liked the Prince and doubted he would be happy to leave his new bride. The two had seemed enamored with each other at the celebration.

Prince Vydall from Vyell was betrothed and not happy about it. The last Enlin had spoken to him, he had listened to the neighboring Prince voice his complaints over his chosen bride- to-be. Apparently, the Lady King Ardal had selected for his son was from across the River of Athadon and was meant to create new alliances. However, that also meant no one knew anything about the future Princess at all.

Enlin allowed his servants to help him dress. Telphee and several guards waited outside of his door. Enlin gave no thought to their presence until they turned to leave the castle. "Where are we going?"

Telphee wrapped a hand firmly around his arm. "Relax, Prince. I am simply following orders."

Something was not right. Enlin scanned the courtyard as they stepped out and into a waiting carriage. Telphee entered with him and sat in the seat across from him. The guards took spots on the back of the carriage, and one with the driver.

"Are we concerned one of the surrounding Royals has brought subterfuge?" The extra entourage of guards made sense for the circumstances. Leaving the castle did not.

"It is a possibility, Prince. We are being cautious."

It was a valid argument. And one Enlin saw no reason not to accept until they pulled up in front of the church. He arched a questioning brow at Telphee.

"This is where the King requested, I bring you, Prince."

Enlin could think of no reason why the King would choose the church. Except one. Enlin curled a hand around the fabric of his cloak, the rich velvet causing a heaviness to gather in his stomach.

They entered through a side door that led into the north transept. The King waited, his face tight and his eyes shadowed. Enlin loosened his fingers. His father's face was grave and shifted the direction his thoughts had gone to consider perhaps his comment of fallacy had been correct.

"Father?" Enlin questioned.

The King waved him forward and Enlin obeyed,

following the rigid stance of his father's back through the doorway that led to the apse. The moment he stepped free into the crossing he saw that his initial conclusion for the deception had been accurate. The Priest stood, hands clasped in front of him, and Breeon stood before him, already in place for the event that had taken from their control.

Guards in full armor blocked any passages that led away, and the church was filled to capacity, the faces expectant and full of excitement as they beamed at their Prince's arrival.

The King faced him, his eyes solemn, his mouth tight. Telphee handed over Enlin's crown, triumph glittering in his eyes.

His father placed the jeweled circle gently on his son's head. "This must be done," he said quietly.

The King maneuvered him forward with a hand on his arm, leaving Enlin no choice but to portray the subservient son who wanted only what was best for his Kingdom. Protesting in front of the people was not an option.

He heard the ripple of whispers and exclamations of enthusiasm that passed through those congregated. Breeon partially turned her head, her face mostly concealed beneath a veil, so he was unable to see her eyes.

At her side, the King raised his son's hand and draped a scarf with the royal emblem of the Lion on it over their wrists, the gesture a symbol of his blessing. He stepped to the side to take his place, allowing the officiant to begin.

The circumstances of a possible threat of war would be enough for anyone to offer grace for the deviations from custom. Having such a strong presence of the Royal Guard would plant enough fear that the threat of attack would easily be taken as an explanation.

Breeon's fingers were cold and stiff beneath his. He had no comfort to offer her and no doubt that she had known as little as he had. There was nothing that either of them could do.

The Priest was reciting the passages from the Bible signifying their commitment to each other. In only minutes, it would be done. Breeon would be his wife.

When would the battle come? Would it be waiting outside of the church doors the moment she was announced as his? Enlin half expected thunder to sound as the Priest continued to drone on.

He was impatient for the order to face his bride and lift the veil. He wanted to see Breeon's eyes. Would she believe he had held no part in tying her to him in this way?

The dictation to face his Princess and make his pledge to her finally came. Enlin did not have the courage to breathe, and it was so quiet he wondered if those gathered held their breaths with him.

He lifted the shield of lace. He did not understand what he saw in her eyes. Standing still and quiet, the words being spoken near them fading, Enlin tried to read the depths of gold. A drum beat inside of his chest that he swore he could hear; a rhythmic beat echoed like the feet of a thousand soldiers.

His lips moved of their own volition as Enlin spoke the words that the Priest directed him to. "I vow to hold you in my heart as my own. To honor the bond God has woven over us on this day as unbreakable. I pledge we are one, united for a purpose greater than we held before, joined together for the good of the Kingdom. As you breathe, I breathe. As long as you shall draw breath, I belong to you, and you belong to me."

Breeon was slow to speak the first words. Each word filled his ears in synchronization with the drum that still beat inside of him. A song swelled, the melody haunting and full of sorrow. Enlin knew no one sang within the church. The music was for him alone and he feared that Alayna sang them, reminding him of the fall of his Kingdom as Breeon declared that he belonged to her.

The kiss Enlin pressed to her lips to seal their union felt like a defeat rather than a victory.

She was his now. Despite all that would come to pass, fate had reached down and decided their futures for them. Breeon was now the future Queen of his Kingdom. However long it reigned.

CHAPTER 18

$\mathcal{N}$o private words were spoken between them. The Royals, nobles and peasants gathered congratulated them and offered and well wishes as they were led from the church. A celebratory feast waited at the castle.

Attendants rode with them in the carriage, making it impossible for them to speak as they fussed over the fall of his cape and the folds of the deep blue gown glittering with jewels that Breeon wore. He wanted to tell her she looked beautiful. Silver strands had been woven into the hair that fell over her shoulders and around her in soft waves.

No thunder had interrupted the silence of the day. No darkness had pushed away the brilliant sun that shone. There was laughter and faces wreathed in smiles on those that raced alongside of the carriage.

Enlin held Breeon's gaze and thought of Prince Gevin. What had been his first thoughts as he had looked into the eyes of his new Princess? He strongly doubted it had been fear and dismay.

Consciously relaxing his face so none would question his commitment to his bride he placed Breeon's hand on top of his as they stepped free of the carriage. A long golden tapestry had been placed over the stone leading into the castle. It was lined with peasants. The nobles and Royals stood alongside it closest to the door. The King and his sisters waited in the wide-open doorway for them.

Breeon was gracious to those that reached out to touch her and congratulate them. She murmured thank you's and took hand after hand as they followed the carpet.

The King waited with his customary dignified stillness.

Kahlee gave Breeon only a cursory glance before smiling at Enlin. "Congratulations, brother. May you and your future Queen long reign." It was a shallow recital with no real sincerity behind it. Kahlee would be far more interested in the attention of the un-betrothed Prince Alpin from Vilitia than she was in her new sister.

Nyala stood at the back where the least amount of people were gathered. Close enough that those beyond the door could see her and know that she honored her brother. The look in her eyes told him she saw his unrest despite his attempts to hide it, but she turned her gaze to Breeon and smiled, holding out a small bouquet of winter foliage.

"I am happy you hold my brother's heart."

Breeon accepted the arrangement. "These are lovely, Nyala. Thank you."

Enlin wanted to tell his sister how stunning she looked in the green dress she wore but was given no chance.

They were led into the Grand Hall. Banquet tables were already laden with food and servants scurried to add more. Ushered forward, the Herald rang a bell, signaling for silence.

The hall had filled by the time they had reached the three thrones that graced the head of the hall. Enlin's head was pounding. He looked out over the gathering, searching for anyone that stood out as a threat.

"Your Royal Majesty, the King!"

The crowd cheered as his father took his throne.

"Your Royal Highness, the Prince!"

Resigned, unable to determine if any of the faces posed a threat, Enlin took his seat.

"Your Royal Highness, the Princess!"

The cheers were deafening as Breeon hesitantly slid into the throne beside his. Enlin could not recall ever seeing the delicately carved golden throne before and wondered if it had been made specifically for Breeon. It suited her, he thought as he watched her settle a hand on the smooth arm of the chair.

She was nervous. Or unsettled. He couldn't tell which. Watching her, he placed his hand over hers and gently curled his fingers over her soft ones. She turned her head to look at him. He was unable to see if his touch brought her any comfort at all.

For hours, they endured the entertainment meant to celebrate their union. They ate, they danced, and they accepted the never-ending congratulations.

Who had put such thought and detail into the revelry to such a degree? Even as Enlin studied the familiar faces that milled near them, he knew. Telphee had done this.

The look on the man's face was enough to convince him. A satisfied sheen gleamed, and his mouth quirked in a proud acceptance of his achievement every time their eyes met.

Enlin was glad of the sword at his side, and the presence of the Royal Guard. Rylan, too, stood by and watched with the fierce steadiness that always took him over whenever he was intensely focused.

The King himself became more strained as the night wore on and the festivities continued. The goblet of wine at his side remained full as he pretended to sip at the contents. Enlin knew his father well enough to sense the tension. The hand resting on the arm of the throne pressed a little too hard against the smooth ivory. His words were a bit short, his smile not far reaching. He did not dance.

It was with great relief that Enlin was finally able to indicate that his new bride should accompany him from the room. The wine had been flowing for long enough that their departure went largely unnoticed.

They walked in silence through the halls, servants trailing them at a respectful distance in case they were needed.

His jaw tightened when he saw that his bedchamber had been invaded during his absence as well. Candles had been lit, a fire laid, and a tray of fruits, cheese and bread set out. A glance into the suite between his room and the adjoining one suggested that it was not vacant any longer.

"Leave us," Enlin ordered, and the servants scurried away with barely concealed snickers.

He didn't hesitate to check that every door and window was securely latched before moving around the room to blow out every candle, leaving only the light from the fire while Breeon stood by and watched his every move.

Enlin had no doubt that she was nervous about his expectations. He indicated the settee in front of the fire, and she sat, curling her fingers around each other and regarding him with an open frankness that surprised him.

It took him a very long minute to determine how to begin. "I was unaware that we were being set up, Breeon. I had no idea until I walked into the church we were about to be married."

She nodded. "I know. I heard Telphee talking, but there was nothing I could do."

"I am sorry, Breeon. I know you did not want this to happen." "It was not supposed to happen," she corrected.

"You say that as though you expected a different outcome?"

"I was very sure that our Creator would not allow it."

"Our Creator?"

She touched a hand to her heart. "The One who guides all life. Do you not believe there is One greater than everything"

Did he tell her he had pondered that very question many times recently? He wanted to understand what she spoke of. "I do not know," he answered honestly.

"Even in the moments I question everything, I hear Him. It is like a calming song that breathes softly if you listen hard enough."

The song he had heard had not calmed him at all. It had struck a chord deep inside that told him the end was near.

"What happens now, Prince Enlin?"

It was a good question, and one he was not sure how to answer. He had devoted plenty of time to thinking about everything but what would happen if he married her.

"I know the marriage cannot be undone. If the predictions we believe are to occur, all we can do is be as prepared as possible." Enlin ran his hand over the smooth hilt of his sword. "Have you ever held a weapon, Breeon?"

"I do not believe so."

Enlin crossed the room to his desk and opened a drawer. Many things had found a home within the desk over the years, and from among the contents he removed a dagger with a single sapphire set in the center of the cross guard.

He had come across the dagger long ago on one of his adventures with Weston and stored it away for safe keeping before forgetting about it. "Rylan can teach you," he said as he handed it to her. "He can get you a garter to conceal it beneath your skirts. Do not go anywhere without it. If we are to find ourselves at war, we need to be mindful at all times. It may well have been easier to keep you safe away from the Kingdom."

Breeon cradled the dagger in her hands, agitation on her face. "It is better to not be afraid of it," he suggested.

"I do not think that I am," she responded, wrapping her hand around the smooth metal handle, and turning her wrist so the blade was aimed for a thrust.

"Are you remembering something?"

"I'm not sure." She rolled her wrist, circling the blade in the air. With a sigh, Breeon set the blade down onto the table beside the settee. "It has been a very long day and I am tired." Her eyes shifted to him, then to the bed before stopping to rest on the fire.

"You needn't fear me, Breeon. You may retire to your own room."

Breeon's lashes lifted slowly as her eyes shifted to his. She studied him for a long time and then stood. "I feel there is much more to say, but I am struggling to make sense of all that is in my head tonight."

"Can you manage on your own? It is best not to call for your Ladies tonight and allow the illusion that everything is..."

"Normal?" Breeon supplied with a small smile.

"Yes."

She nodded and stood, moving toward the door to the sitting area set between their suites.

"Lady Breeon."

She turned back and Enlin held up the dagger she had left behind. "Sleep with it beside you, please. And do not shut the adjoining doors so I can hear you if you call."

The layers of her skirts moved prettily around her as she walked back. He was sure the dress had been made quickly, but it complemented her well. He wanted to tell her but couldn't seem to find the right words.

Enlin forgot about the dagger in his hand. There was only her.

"Who can guess at the plans of God?" she whispered as she looked up at him.

"God? The Creator you spoke of?" Her eyes glittered in the firelight. He was as mesmerized by them as he was by her words.

"Do you not believe that His Hand is upon us? There

must be a purpose to how we have come to this place, despite all odds, and have found ourselves united?"

"You speak in riddles."

"I do not mean to, Prince Enlin. My heart and mind speak, and I have only to seek beyond myself to feel a complexity at work that astounds me."

"More riddles, my Princess," Enlin said quietly and taking her hand, he lifted it and put the handle of the dagger into her palm.

"The morning will be better for such words," he said, letting go of the softness of her hand reluctantly.

CHAPTER 19

A hand upon his shoulder woke him. Rylan peered down at him when Enlin opened bleary eyes to faint morning light. "What?"

"Fetch your bride. The Grandmaster waits disturbed and shaken."

Throwing aside the covers, Enlin hurried through his morning ministrations and dressed.

He was hesitant to enter Breeon's chambers but knew that it was better for Rylan to have awakened him before the servants came and discovered the new Princess had not shared her new husband's bed.

He was surprised to find her already dressed and curled up on the window seat that faced the west. "Did you sleep?" he asked.

Her eyes were wide and bright, faint shadows beneath them. "Enlin... I am afraid of what comes."

Enlin went to her side quickly, placing a hand on her shoulder to peer past her beyond the windowpane. "What is it that you see?"

She wrapped cold fingers around his and pressed his

hand over her heart. "I see it here. I cannot explain it... like tiny pieces of me are being torn from my soul. It is painful."

Enlin took her face in his hands. He could see faint signs of her discomfort in the gold of her eyes. "You are in pain now?"

"What does it mean?" she pleaded, and the distress in her voice caused a surge of fierce protectiveness to rise, like one of the roaring lions that graced the castle.

"I will make it stop," he promised her fervently, and straightened. "Rylan!"

Rylan appeared quickly. Enlin assumed he had stood on the other side of the doorway to give them some privacy.

"War is coming."

Striding to stand beside his Prince, Rylan examined the lands beyond the glass. "I see nothing."

"She does not see it there."

There was no disbelief on Rylan's face as he turned his gaze to the Princess. "The Knights have already been called. Come, Prince, the Council waits," he stated and spun to leave.

"Come, Princess," Enlin said softly and Breeon slid her hand into his and rose, squeezing tightly. He looked down at her for a few moments, remembering her words of God. If there was one, he hoped that she was being cared for. He did not know how to take away pain that came from the inside. "I must find a way to get you to safety, and my sisters as well."

"I can fight." Her words were tremulous, but there was courage in them.

"I'd rather you stay alive," Enlin replied.

"Your confidence in my abilities has merit as you have never seen me fight, but somehow I have determined that I can." She released his hand, and he watched as she went to the chaise lounge set at the end of her bed. The dagger was there and Breeon picked it up, spinning the handle in her palm.

The jewel glinted as she walked back. "There is a time for war," she murmured as she fell back into step beside him. She said it with conviction and a slight lift to her chin. He wondered if memories were surfacing. Her brow was drawn, her eyes intent on the weapon.

"I can fight," she whispered. Her eyes lifted to his, intensity firing the gold flecks in her eyes. "I will fight. Am I not your wife now? Does that not mean that I must protect the Kingdom the same way you would protect it?" She shifted her shoulders back, her chin lifting another fraction. "These are now my people as well."

Breeon was challenging him, but Enlin could not formulate words to convey what he felt as a result of hearing them. His Kingdom had always meant everything to him, and here his new wife was, accepting the same blessing and burden as though it had always been hers as well.

Was it pride if he refused her? Or part of his need to protect her?

He gave a slight nod. She was right. They were now her people. "We must outfit you properly then. And you must prove to me that you do know how to handle that dagger. First, we meet with the Council."

"She will not be allowed," Rylan said over his shoulder as they rounded the last corner to the Council Chambers.

"Breeon is the future Queen of Kingdom Silvera. She will sit at my side where she belongs," Enlin stated firmly as they entered.

Telphee shot to his feet at the sight of his new bride. Enlin held up his hand. "Not one word," he snapped. "You placed her in this position, but I far outrank you, and she will stay."

Rylan positioned himself behind the chair he directed Breeon to and crossed his arms, daring Telphee to make an attempt.

Enlin took his own seat beside the King, who nodded at the GrandMaster. "What is it that calls us here so early this morning?"

"Your Majesty, scouts have returned from the North. An army marches for us."

So, it would come to pass. Enlin had hoped the scouts would all return with news that peace remained. It was not to be so. "And the other scouts?" he inquired.

"Have not yet returned, Your Highness."

Enlin nodded. The Kingdom was well on its way to being fully armed and ready for battle, as were those around them.

His grandfather had been wise with his alliances. Each Kingdom had enough men to defend their walls. Their enemy would have no way of knowing they had fortified Silvera based on prophecy.

The Knights that had served under the previous King were solemn. They had seen death, experienced the sorrow of taking a life, and spent far too much time bearing the long days that stretched into months while men and hope died.

Enlin had heard their stories. Even the loss of one of his men was too many. He did not want war.

"Whose army marches upon us?" the King asked.

The GrandMaster glanced away, not soon enough to hide the fear that bloomed dark and bright. "They bear the emblem of the Kingdom of Aviore, Your Majesty... and there are...men... from the Fallen Valley."

"Aviore?" The King broke in. "They are a quiet Kingdom, small, with little power. That makes no sense at all. The revolt must be led by those in the Fallen Valley."

Which explained the Grandmaster's fear. No one entered the Fallen Valley and returned, and the narratives associated with the place were all dark and sinister. As far as Enlin was aware, it was nothing more than a valley steeped in super-stition.

"I know little of either," Enlin commented. He could

114

recall only a few times he had heard mention of the Kingdom of Aviore at all. It was just outside of the north border of the allied Kingdoms and as his father had said, it was too small to form any army large enough to take on a Kingdom of their size.

The King shoved back his chair and rose, pacing over the stone, his cloak billowing over the woven rug beneath his feet. "They have no hope of victory. Perhaps we can resolve this after all." The pacing stopped abruptly, and the King pierced the Herald with his gaze. "I will send a message and tell them to stop, or we will be forced to fight. They must know the odds are against them."

"We should not allow them to reach the Kingdom," Enlin said. "We have the advantage. We can call for Ovsia and Vyell to meet us with their companies and gain a victory before they ever reach the walls."

"Vyell will need extra fortification first. The mountains to the west will force the army to choose between the road that leads here or to bring the battle to Vyell. We can't leave them vulnerable." The King had resumed his pacing.

"If they manage to take Vyell, I would imagine they would continue south. They would have towns to contend with, but between us and them there would be no one to challenge them."

Enlin could argue with nothing. His father was right. Ovsia was west of the mountains, and Vilitia was south beyond the Kingdom. There were many vulnerable towns scattered outside of the walls of the castles throughout the land, and other Kingdoms further away would be unable to send aid quickly over the distance between them.

"They have no other options," the King continued. "We need to call up arms from Vilitia and have Ovsia block them. If all our Kingdoms meet beyond the border of the Woods of Valoria, we can end this there."

Enlin hesitated to remind his father that both prophecies

they had held secret for so long had stated that their Kingdom would fall, not any of the others around them. Could they change what had been spoken?

The Herald entered and sat to take down the messages that would be sent to their allies.

It would not be long before Enlin knew he would find himself facing an enemy that meant to try to destroy everything he knew and loved. He hoped when the time came, he would not be the cause of the end of his Kingdom.

That was something he could not bear. It was a sobering thought that perhaps Alayna had seen something in him that had made him believe he would not change his path. Was his father changing his?

"What is it that they want?"

All eyes turned to Breeon.

"Princess?" The King was obviously startled that she had spoken. Enlin prepared himself to offer support if it was needed. No one had asked the question she had.

"If their army is small and the chance at victory is as well, why would they try? There must be something here that they want."

"Princess Breeon, I mean no respect, but you know nothing of war," the GrandMaster interjected. "They intend to gain power."

"At what cost?" Breeon exclaimed. "Why from here? Why not just this Kingdom of Vyell you speak of if that is all they seek?" Her eyes snapped to the King. "Your Kingdom is the one that I see crumbling."

"What treason is this?" Telphee demanded, shooting up from his chair. "You must be silent, Princess!"

Enlin stood, silencing Telphee with a look. He placed his hand on Breeon's shoulder. "She is right. We must consider what they hope to gain by bringing an army against any of the Kingdom's? We cannot know their destination or their intent."

He looked at his father. Both knew it was Silvera. Those in the Council did not need to know the why. He looked around at each of the Knights gathered. They waited silently for him to speak, their loyalty in their lack of protest.

The King did not attempt to take back their focus. Enlin would delve into the reasoning for that later. "I will take an Order of Knights and ride out to meet this army. If peace is an option, I want to offer it. If it is not, I want to know why."

Decision made, Enlin waved a hand to signal the meeting was over and held out a hand to Breeon. She took it and stood, and he led her from the room.

"I am sorry I cause you distress," she apologized when they were away from any listening ears.

"You cause me no distress, Breeon. Your words were well spoken and needed to be considered. The Kingdom is unused to having a future Queen. They will need to adapt."

He turned to Rylan. "Breeon needs to be outfitted properly to fight. I will take her to the kitchens for breakfast and meet you in the Armory."

Rylan nodded and left them.

"Did you see more of... the things you see... in my father's eyes?"

Breeon shook her head. "No, but the shadows are still there. Your father is troubled by a great burden."

Enlin opened his mouth to tell her of the angel wing tale but closed it again. How silly such a story was. He needed to concentrate on what was real.

A glance at the woman beside him was enough to convince him of that. He would do whatever it took to keep her safe.

CHAPTER 20

*R*ylan had done as he was asked.

At his presence, the Armorer abandoned the Knights he was outfitting to rush to meet them.

"Your Highness." He was greeted with a quick bow and motioned into the Royal Armory rooms. "Your armor is ready."

Knights, archers, and squires were being readied. The armory was bustling with soldiers being outfitted for war. The castle grounds were loud with shouted orders, the whinnies and clop of horse hooves, and the march of men. They were not sounds that Enlin had ever wanted to hear for such a purpose. Not while he called his homeland his own.

With an army heading their way, precautionary measures had become honed into targeted detail. Armor would not be worn at all times by those prepared to fight. Another small detail that had become necessary.

"The Princess needs protection, as well."

Inside of the stone room that housed the royal armor, the Armorer looked at him in confusion. "Your Highness?"

"She will fight," Enlin clarified.

The man gaped for a moment before regaining control of

his facilities. "Of course, of course," he muttered and cast a panicked look around the room, his hands splayed out at his sides. It would have been comical if the circumstances had not been what they were. He shouted for assistance and grabbed at a pair of greaves, holding them out to the Prince.

Enlin accepted them and sat to put them on. While the Armorer aided him in dressing for battle, the man directed the boys who had come at his bidding, ordering them to bring options in for Breeon to try on for fit.

Dividing his time between the two of them, he muttered to himself as piece after piece was rejected, until he was finally happy with a thin metal breastplate, leather gauntlets, and pauldron's. "Your Highness, forgive me, but it is no good to send her out with ill-fitting armor. If she cannot move comfortably, it could mean her death."

"I understand," Enlin agreed. "The battle may not come today. I expect you will work hard to create something more fitting for the Princess?"

"Of course, Your Highness." The Armorer swept into a bow. "Princess, allow me to show you the weapons at your disposal?"

The Armorer selected a key from the ring at his side and unlocked another room that held the royal arms. The stone walls were adorned with swords, bows, spears, and other various weapons meant for battle.

Enlin slid his favored sword into the sheath at his side, hanging the one he carried with him every day. Breeon slowly walked the length of wall, eyeing longswords, crossbows, and halberds. She bypassed them all and moved to a line of chests set along one wall.

Walking to one, she placed her hand on top. Enlin watched her fingers splay over the wood, her head tilt. He saw her lashes flutter down and a tremble flitter over her shoulders.

"Princess?" The Armorer helped her to lift the heavy lid.

Enlin knew that weapons were kept in the chests, but not what they were. He had always been told they were of no use to him. Straw fell to the floor.

"These are what I want," Breeon murmured as a long, scarred wooden box was lifted out. The Armorer glanced at Enlin, an odd look of caution in his eyes. Enlin stepped forward to watch as the lid was lifted.

Inside were two short swords, the metal glistening as though freshly polished. The cross guards were gold, spanned out in the shape of wings, and the each of the hilts were intricately embossed. "Do you have a back scabbard for these?" she asked.

Enlin arched a brow. "Breeon?" he questioned. How could she possibly know that terminology? She took the swords from the box and held one in each hand. She turned to face him, a smile on her face. Gold flecks danced, light making them shine. It had to be from the reflection of the swords.

"I am a warrior," she stated, the knowledge confident in her words, her stance and hold on the munitions indicating that it was true.

One of the boys had fetched a scabbard and the Armorer secured it for Breeon. She slipped the swords into the thick leather. "I am ready."

The boy stared at her, clearly entranced. The Armorer's thick brows were drawn into a disapproving scowl. Enlin could not hide his smile. A woman dressed as a warrior was not common. He could recall no recollection of his own of ever seeing one. There were, of course, stories woven around women who fought fiercely, but none had ever declared the tales as truth.

He admired her assuredness. He himself did not feel the same. As a Prince, he had trained for the possibility of such a day coming but facing opponents who wanted to kill those he cared about versus one for training was a frightening difference.

Rylan stepped into the room and swept his eyes over Breeon. "Lady Breeon, may I urge you to reconsider what you are preparing to do?"

"Joining the battle?"

"Yes," Rylan said, contemplating her. He could see no fear in her eyes. Behind her, Enlin was apprehensive. "Let us engage in a bit of a... practice battle, hmm, Princess?" he suggested.

Breeon nodded and followed him as Rylan led the way into the training yard. Those not engaged in other activities began to gather immediately at the sight of them squaring off.

Enlin watched Breeon pull the swords from the scabbard as though she had done it hundreds of times before, holding them loosely in her hands as she took a position facing Rylan.

A smile of anticipation curved her lips. She rolled one of the swords in her hand. Enlin did not miss the quick tightening of her lower fingers on the hilt as Rylan pulled his own sword.

"Seems an unfair fight, Princess, that the reach of my sword will keep you at bay."

The smile widened. "Rylan, I'm quite sure you should never underestimate your opponent, no matter how balanced you feel the odds are weighted."

She moved, a quick, graceful shift of her feet that dropped her body and transitioned her to Rylan's left, leaving his side free for her to thrust her sword to pause it just a breadth from sinking into his rib cage.

The crowd gathered gasped. A few distinctly female voices rose in a cheer. Rylan arched a brow and gave an approving nod to Breeon. "My mistake, Princess. I did exactly as you suggested I should not do."

Breeon trailed the tip of her blade lightly over the leather covering Rylan wore as she walked around his body, taunting him. "The metal is warm in my hand, the feel of it exhilaratingly familiar. I believe I have found a part of myself I had forgotten."

"Confidence can make one both deadly and over-zealous."

The smile and mischievous teasing died and Breeon resumed her stance in preparation to fight. "I can say confidently, Rylan, that I am not an over-zealous warrior."

This time, it was Rylan who made the first move. The two danced around each other, but each swing of the heavier sword was met with a parry of the shorter.

Rylan was a trained fighter and had built stamina from his years of practice. Enlin expected Breeon to tire quickly, but the glint and determination that had taken over the soft banter of before remained. Thrust, counter, swing, the two matched each other, despite the variance in size and weaponry.

It was in Rylan that Enlin first noticed the signs of strain. Enlin knew him well enough to know that it would only spark a churning of fierceness in battle. A last attempt to obtain victory had won him more than one fight on the training field.

There was power behind his next onslaught, and the result cast away one of Breeon's short swords. Mud spattered around the blade as it fell to the ground. Rylan did not hesitate, but moved forward with deadly intent, pushing Breeon back so she was forced to kneel as she used her remaining weapon to protect herself from the blow.

Triumph quirked a corner of Rylan's mouth, and so focused was he on waiting for Breeon to concede that he missed the subtle movement of her free hand releasing the dagger from beneath her skirts until it was thrust up, so the tip was pressed against his belly.

Shock drowned the triumph and widened Rylan's eyes as he looked down to see that he had lost. He pulled back his sword and straightened, staring at the woman below him.

Enlin waited with all the others for Rylan's reaction to the loss. To a woman. Never mind that it was the Princess. None would believe he had allowed her win.

Sliding his blade into the sheath at his side, Rylan held out a hand. Breeon slowly slipped the dagger back into its garter, and the short sword she still held into the scabbard before accepting the hand and standing. Mud clung to the violet skirt she wore, smudging out the pattern beneath.

"I would be proud, and honored, to have you on the battlefield at our side, Princess." Rylan bowed low. His words were as earnest as the grip on her hand.

Applause began. Enlin stepped into the yard and retrieved the second short sword, handing it to the woman who had just surprised him yet again. "I cannot think where you have learned to fight like that," he said to her quietly.

Rylan heard. "Your body remembered how to fight; has your mind remembered anything as well?"

Breeon shook her head. "I'm sorry, but no." She sighed, the sound one of satisfaction and not of frustration as she slid the weapon handed to her into place beside the other. "However, that was... enjoyable. Thank you, Rylan, for allowing me the opportunity to prove myself."

"I'm afraid I'll never live it down," Rylan responded drily. "Come, we have dawdled enough. We have a Kingdom to save."

CHAPTER 21

By nightfall, the Knights that had been chosen to accompany Enlin to meet the forthcoming army had been gathered and prepped for an early departure.

Enlin had spent the day seeing to details; organizing, strategizing, and planning for every possible route and scenario that could be thought of. He had not seen Breeon since the morning in the Armory. He had heard plenty of comments about it, and a few had even apologetically offered their advice against allowing Breeon to set foot on any battlefield.

She would not go with him to the frontline to meet the army. Enlin had spent several hours of the day setting plans in place to protect the women and children within the castle walls if a breach occurred, and both Breeon and his sisters had been a central focus.

"Enlin."

Turning at his name, Enlin saw his father in the doorway of his private chamber. Concealing a sigh, Enlin backtracked away from his own chambers to accommodate the beckoning.

Inside, the door closed behind them, the King looked his

son over. Seeing his son outfitted for battle had not been something he had ever wanted. "I have concerns. Telphee told me of the incident in the yards this morning. I fear you are not making wise decisions."

Enlin crossed his arms.

"Have you forgotten the entire point of taking a wife is to produce an heir?"

The words sounded like they had come straight from Telphee's mouth. Enlin clenched his jaw, wondering what else Telphee had filled the King's ears with. "I disagree. A wife is far more than a breeder."

"Putting her on a battlefield does the Kingdom no good. Nor do I care for the message it sends to the women of the Kingdom."

"You don't like it, or Telphee doesn't like it? She is courageous and placing herself at my side on the battlefield upholds the vows we spoke in the church. 'United for a purpose greater than we held before.' Her loyalty and bravery astound me."

The King shook his head. "You are enamored. This... this entrancement she has over you makes you blind. She could still well be part of a plot to bring down the Kingdom. What words has she used to guide the direction you have chosen?"

"Have you forgotten the Council agreed to our plans? Breeon does not lead this war. She simply stands at my side. She shows the people that she will be a Queen who holds her people's safety and happiness as closely as her own."

"She is not yet the Queen!" the King exploded.

Enlin took a step toward his father. "What is it that you fear so greatly from her? Is it that she sees beyond what you show your people? Or is it your own choices that are causing this defense?"

"Careful, my son. I am still your King."

"Are you forbidding her to join me in battle?"

The King was silent. His eyes were hooded, his breathing

slow and deep through his nose. Enlin felt a frisson of unease. Was there still more his father had withheld from him?

"I am not," the King said, the words low and hard. "Telphee is not wrong. Lady Breeon holds value. If we win this war, Enlin, it does us no good if there is no heir. You must consider the importance of this." Bitterness twisted the King's next words. "Marriage has few joys. Finding your pleasure is one of them. You could try taking it a bit more seriously and have some fun while you are at it."

"At what expense?" Enlin shook his head in disgust. "I hardly know the woman. I will not gain her trust by forcing myself upon her. Nor will it begin my marriage in a way I care for. Telphee needs to learn to hold his tongue."

Walking to the wall lined with portraits of Kings, his father lifted a hand to touch the bottom of the frame that depicted the previous King. "Enlin, I have found that one of the hardest lessons I have tried to teach you is that as King, your word and your command, dictates the outcome. You so easily bend to the persuasion of another, and this is your greatest fault."

The criticism struck Enlin like a blow. His father did not often offer such critical insights. Was it true? Did he allow the words of others to sway him? Was there a specific instance being referred to?

He thought of Telphee and the ploy that had brought them to where they were. "Are you saying I should have defied Telphee and not married Breeon?"

Pivoting, the King scowled at his son. "No! You have waited far too long to marry, and I allowed it. As my only son, perhaps I placated your wishes when I should not have. Marrying was your duty." Sweeping the folds of his cloak aside to sit, the King continued.

"Allowing the feelings and emotions of your new bride to let things happen that violate duty are what I speak of.

Giving her a dagger to carry is one thing; letting her believe she can live against a man with a sword is another."

He held up a hand when Enlin opened his mouth. "Waiting for her to feel comfortable with you before you make your marriage real is misguided. As the future King, you need to realize that convention is different. We do not marry for love. If you wait for an emotion to happen that does not even exist, this Kingdom will die with you."

Hearing the jaded base the King lectured out of saddened Enlin. His father could do nothing about what happened behind closed doors. The advice he was being given would not change the choices he had made. Nor would he take the swords or armor from Breeon. He believed that she was a fighter. He had seen her in action.

More than that, there was something in him that desired the kind of wife she was presenting herself to be. A strong woman who defied fear and faced it head on. One who put others who were no more than strangers to her before her own safety. One who was not what his father spoke of.

Led by emotion and feeling, Breeon lived and spoke what was in her heart. Molding her into the kind of woman his father was referring to would destroy her.

"Do you really not believe in love? What of Alayna? Did you love her?"

The King scoffed. "Love. It is only an illusion taught in fairy tales. Lust. Desire. Want. Need. Duty. Those things are real. They dictate actions every day. Love? What does a claim of love do? It destroys people. Kingdoms. No, I do not believe in such a thing. Nor should you."

"What of compassion? Grace, generosity, mercy? What of those feelings?" For the first time, Enlin felt the coldness of his father's gaze slice into him. Had the man before him done nothing but raise him out of duty? He could not ask for the assurance he suddenly needed to hear. He was too afraid of the answer.

Was that why he had been so drawn to Breeon? From the start it had been obvious that she cared about people. She was kind to animals, to his sister, to Rylan. What more would he learn about her as the days passed?

"Don't answer that," Enlin said, lifting a hand. He didn't want to learn any more about the man who had created him. Thinking back to Breeon's talk about God, Enlin thought about how nice it would be to believe there was someone waiting to listen, someone who would never let him down. At least, those were things he recalled the Priest saying. It was possible the Priest was saying things just to make those listening feel better.

"I have to go," he announced. It had been a very long day and sitting in front of the fire in his suite and shutting down his mind for awhile was exactly what he needed.

"Think about what I've said, Enlin," his father requested as he left the room.

Enlin didn't bother giving an answer. Not thinking at all was his plan.

Until he walked into his chamber and saw Breeon waiting on his settee in front of the fire. "Breeon."

It was late. He had been sure she would have been sleeping. "Rylan told me I will be staying here."

"You're upset with me because of it?"

She shook her head, leaning forward to pour wine into a goblet. "Velynn asked your Chamberlain what you prefer before you retire," she explained, handing over the cup.

Kindness, Enlin thought again. "That was considerate of you."

"I have tried to imagine what it would be like to ride out to meet the army that marches to try and destroy everything that you love. I cannot. Rylan explained it is too soon to place me at your side. That it is better for them to not know my face." "He is right." Deciding it was best to keep distance between them, Enlin sat in one of the chairs to the side of the settee.

He stretched his feet out toward the fire, sighing with pleasure at the heat and soothing flames.

"Are you afraid?"

Enlin chuckled. Of course, she would ask such a question. "Men try not to speak of such feelings."

"I am afraid."

His mirth died a quick death. "Of what, Breeon?"

Her eyes flared golden in the firelight. "That you won't come back."

CHAPTER 22

*T*here was little talking among the Knights as they departed on their horses through the castle gates. They had a mission and all of them knew what they left behind could not split their focus.

Versiah Road would carry them between the Woods of Valoria and Silvanna, where his cabin was located. From there, the Osval Mountains would be to the West and Kingdom Vyell would be the the East. A small town, Verton was just beyond the walls of Vyell and would be an easy target for an army looking to make a statement.

It was the hope that they would meet the army before any blood was spilled. Verton was the last town before Versiah Road forked, leading one either to Kingdom Aviore or the Fallen Valley.

The journey would take longer than the light of the day. They would camp to the south of Vyell and join the Knights there before adding to their number and continuing.

Enlin could feel a hint of the dying winter on the exposed skin of his arms, but the sun was bright and warmed him. Mud clung to the horses' legs as they galloped over the road.

The forests were behind them, the stretching expanse of

Oak, Beech and Spruce of the Silvanna comforting in its familiarity. The long miles it had taken to pass had given Enlin plenty of time to compare the differences between the two.

Neither were close to the road, but if one were to seek shelter, the Silvanna at least looked passable. The woods of Valoria did not. Enlin knew only that the trees nearest the road and scattered throughout the perimeter of Valoria were called Angel Oak. The spreading branches dissuaded anyone from entering, the tentacle-like wood twining and spiraling in odd formations creating a near impassable wall.

He had not noticed before that boulders looked as though they had fallen to add to the discouraging landscape. It made far more sense for the boulders to be along the Silvanna, as the mountains were closer there.

Enlin wondered of Alayna as they passed by her home. Did she know of the advancing army? Was she concerned for her Kingdom? It would be settling to discover her motivations. The time they had spent with her had been short, and not enough to lend him any true conclusions of her character.

Near mid-day Enlin felt suddenly as though something were wrong. His fingers tightened on the reins, and he scanned the horizon sharply. Signaling for those near him to be on alert, he continued to search for the cause of his unrest.

He saw nothing out of place. It would not be long before they reached where the road crossed over the River of Athadon. It was there that they planned to set up camp for the night and allow the horses to rest.

The southern border of Vyell was nestled at the banks of the river where it forked to the east and west. Passing over the bridge would give them access to the road that led east to the province and if they had beaten the army, their company would find themselves at the gates before the sun had risen fully in the sky.

His disquiet stayed with him. Enlin posted guards and sent out scouts as camp was set up. There was nowhere for an army to hide from them. The river offered water and fish. Around the banks there was nothing but open land and a clear horizon for miles.

The Knights knew well enough that he was anxious. There was no joviality as horses were cared for and food was cooked. The tight lines on the faces of the older Knights and hands kept close to sword hilts gave the younger soldiers apprehension of their own. There would be little sleep that night as all reflected on what the following day would bring.

"Eat, Prince Enlin. It does you no good to dwell on things that have not happened."

Accepting the plate Rylan held out, Enlin nodded and forced himself to do as suggested.

"Breeon is fine," Rylan commented as he sat across from his Prince.

Would he know if she was not? Thinking of her made the pit in his stomach heavier. Enlin dropped his fork to his plate. "Something is wrong, Rylan." He lifted his eyes, looking back toward the Kingdom. Rylan was wrong. Breeon was not fine.

Enlin stood, uncertain of his actions. He could not abandon his men to go back.

"Your Highness!"

He turned at the call. Sham, one of the scouts, had returned and the look on his face was grim. He reined his horse a stop, the abrupt move sinking the horse's hooves into the soft ground. Mud spattered as the scout's boots hit the ground.

"Your Highness, Kingdom Vyell burns!"

Was it not Breeon then? Enlin refrained from pressing a hand to his churning stomach. The news did not calm the weight he felt.

"We are too late," Rylan stated. He flagged a passing

soldier. "Gather the Silver Knights and bring them to the Prince's tent," he ordered.

Enlin's mind whirled as he waited for the Knights' arrival. Where was the army now if Vyell had already fallen? Or if it was currently under attack, did they break camp and go on? Darkness would soon come and make the journey dangerous.

And Breeon. Where did he put her in all of this? She was in danger. He could feel it.

Rylan touched his arm and Enlin faced the Knights that had earned the highest rank given by his Kingdom. They had proven their loyalty and their abilities were unmatched. The scout waited to answer the questions that had not yet been asked. Two scouts had been sent to Vyell. Sham along the road, and the other along the river.

"How far did you go?"

"I could see the road that leads to Vyell, Your Highness. The smoke was visible from there and I turned back."

Enlin nodded. "Verton?"

"I could see it in the distance, Your Highness. All looked well."

"The scout that brought news of the army said they followed Versiah Road. They must have left its path to take a direct route to Vyell, bypassing Verton."

Pacing, remembering the King's words that he was too easily led by his emotions, Enlin questioned the plan he had formulated while waiting for the Knights. Was it the wrong one? He blew out a breath, realizing he was mimicking the habit his father demonstrated in distress.

He stopped where he was and pierced Rylan with a look. Rylan would know to counter his decision if needed. He trusted Rylan and the man had never held back if he felt Enlin was off base.

"Sham, take another scout and head back toward the

Kingdom. I want word that Princess Breeon, my sisters and the Kingdom are well." The scout nodded and departed.

"If the army is in Vyell, we must head them off before they reach passage over the river. We will break camp at dawn and make our way toward Vyell. We will wait for the second scout to report before we make further plans."

Rylan gave a slight dip of his head, indicating that he agreed.

"Prepare the Second Order of Knights. If the river is clear, they will go tonight to offer aid."

Garin, the Grandmaster, nodded. "Immediately, Your Highness." His departure signaled for the others to follow.

"The men need to be warned they must be ready," Enlin said to Rylan.

"Rest, Prince. I will see to it." Rylan studied him for a few moments. "If I may, I do believe fate can be changed. Our choices and our actions are what determine our destiny. Nothing you have done has been reckless or unwarranted. You must have confidence that you can save your Kingdom. Whatever Alayna said, she is no god. Her words are not set in stone."

Rylan did not wait for Enlin to answer but left to prepare the soldiers for the war that waited on the morrow.

Enlin hoped Rylan was right. He settled on his pallet but knew that he would not sleep. Wrapping his hand around the hilt of his sword, he traced the pattern with his thumb. He had never taken the life of another. Would he be forced to?

He thought of Viker, the ruler of Aviore. What did the man want? Why had he not sought a peaceful resolution before bringing an army against those that had considered him an ally? Did his father know the reason? Had that been part of the reason for the shadows in his eyes?

Viker was unknown to him by anything other than name and what he knew from a few comments during Council meetings. The Kingdom was small and held little significance. Perhaps the man craved power, but Enlin did not see how he hoped to gain it without a large army at his disposal. He would be far outnumbered.

The Knights of Vyell would not shift their allegiance. That left the occupants of the Fallen Valley. Were they numbered to give Aviore the advantage? Enlin did not see how that was possible. Would they not know more about the place if there was any substance to it?

Could a Kingdom have been built without their knowledge within the mysterious depths? Shaking his head on the soft fur, Enlin closed his eyes, thinking of the descriptions he had been told of the stone cliffs that rose and fell into a void. No one knew what was below the drop off. The precipice's rose to great heights and then fell off into nothing. The canyon itself was long and wide and nothing grew in the gray dirt that makes the territory of the Valley.

There was no life there. The men spoken of in the tales of the place were believed to be fictitious for the most part. Those that did believe in their existence thought them evil.

Logically, Aviore was alone or had gathered affiliations with Kingdoms far from Silvera. Or, he was concerned for nothing, and the war would be won before any had really begun at all.

That notion brought some comfort, and he gave his thoughts over to Breeon. His overwrought and exhausted mind hovered there, the faint strain of a song beginning deep in his soul. It was tinged in pain and stuttered over the notes, but still, it was beautiful and soothing, and Enlin slept.

CHAPTER 23

*I*t was only a shifting of soft ground beneath feet, but it woke him. Enlin's sword was in his hand as he sprung from his bed.

Alayna stood before him, a dark cloak covering her. The fire burned low, but he recognized the blue of her eyes and the sheen of her hair beneath the circle of her hood.

A quick glance told him they were alone. "How did you get past the guards?"

"Prince Enlin." Alayna removed her hood and moved forward as he sheathed his sword. "I was wrong. You have changed your fate."

"What are you talking about?"

"I was in the village, and I heard some of the peasants talking. It meant nothing to me until I was shown..."

"Speak clearly, Alayna. I have little patience left."

Alayna rushed forward and reached out to grasp his hands. He stared at her, seeing the same bright, mesmerizing light he remembered the first time she had spoken words over him that had changed his life.

"Princess Breeon was not the woman you married in my

first vision. You heeded my warning. Your bride will not cause your Kingdom to fall."

He took a few moments to contemplate what she said. "Why are you telling me this now? A war has begun, Alayna."

"You don't understand," she breathed fervently. "I was so tired yesterday and finally I gave in, and I slept. I saw so many things! Lady Breeon. She is in danger and so is Nyala! You must go back!"

Enlin pulled his hands free and stepped away from her. "How do you know it was not Breeon? You were very certain that if I married, the Kingdom would fall, and it has already begun."

She shook her head. "No. Not because of her. In the vision, her dress was the color of fresh milk, not the dark blue the townspeople speak of. Her hair was as dark as granite, not gilded with the kiss of the sun. Nor did she smile in triumph when she faced those gathered. Rather, they say Lady Breeon looked at them as though they had become hers."

"So, you are telling me I married the wrong woman?"

"Prince Enlin, please, it matters not what I saw before! It is the things I was shown as the dark of night fell that you must listen to!"

"Did you tell my father that if an angel feather was found in the forest, it would bring about the end of the Kingdom?"

"Yes! All these years I have known this would come, but I had hoped and prayed that it could somehow be changed. It was not until I realized your part in this did change that I heard the song again. It swelled in my spirit and filled me for a few moments, and I felt joy and peace again. I clung to that, Prince Enlin, until the exhaustion claimed me."

Tears glistened in her eyes and fell. Her hands trembled and he watched her clasp them. "He has done nothing to change, and I felt her pain as their feet crushed the chords of the song. I remember that pain so well." Her eyes closed, her features twisting. "Go back, Prince Enlin," she murmured with her eyes still pressed shut. "Save them both."

Enlin closed the distance between them. "Alayna," he said firmly. Her eyes opened, shiny and haunted.

"What do you know of Breeon? And what does Nyala have to do with any of this?"

She shook her head. "I have said too much already." Another tear trailed a slow path down her cheek.

The tension in his stomach had clenched as she had given him her warning. Enlin was torn between duty and his feelings. Just as his father had said. His duty was to accompany his men to the battlefield. His heart told him he needed to heed Alayna's foresight and return to home to protect those he held in his heart.

"Beneath the feet of my enemy, the feathers would be trampled." Enlin recalled his father's recollection of the prophecy Alayna had allegedly given to him. "Is that what you speak of? Are you aware that angels are mythical creatures?"

"Does the King not hold a feather in his possession as we speak?" Alayna demanded, the words shaky with her emotions.

His breath caught in his lungs, captured just above the weight that was threatening to make him sick. He considered the wings of the iridescent butterflies, the strange twisting limbs of the trees in Valoria, and latched on to the sparkle of gold he had seen more than once in Breeon's eyes.

He stared at Alayna in shock. She backed up, retreating toward the back wall of the tent. "If one has the eyes to see, Prince Enlin, the heart can settle on what it believes."

Realizing she was leaving, Enlin started after her. "Alayna, wait!" She had already slipped beneath the flap of the tent, her smaller stature making it easy for her. Enlin struggled with it, his armor and sword prohibiting him from following her.

Striding to the entrance of his tent, he exited, startling the posted guards. "Your Highness?"

"Prepare my horse!" Enlin shouted as he rounded the tent.

Two Knights flanked him, swords drawn. "What is it, Your Highness?"

Enlin scanned the rows of tents surrounding his. He did not see her. How had she slipped unnoticed through the camp? Why had she felt she could tell him no more? Was someone watching her? Guiding her actions?

He spun. "I need to return to the Kingdom immediately. Has the second scout returned?"

"No, Your Highness." Armen, one of the Silver Knights slid his sword back into its hold. "We sent the Second Order and the Third is ready to fight if needed."

Alayna had given him what he needed. His instinct told him to listen. He shoved away the admonition of the King that had shadowed every decision since it had been spoken over him. "Vyell was a decoy. The army will be upon Silvera soon. Break camp immediately. We will not wait for dawn."

Within the hour, torches had been lit and the sound of horse's hooves filled the night air as they began the journey back to their Kingdom. Another scout had been sent to meet the Second Order of Knights to instruct them to bring any left from Vyell that were able to fight to join them.

They rode hard and fast until the leading Knights stopped the procession. "What?" Enlin demanded, drawing his horse alongside the two that had ridden back to meet him.

"You'll want to see this, Your Highness."

He and Rylan spurred their horses to move to follow the men to the front line of the company. Enlin dismounted on the road, staring at what was ahead.

What once had been nothing but gravel and stone was now littered with wood that had been hacked to pieces. Enlin trailed a broken path to the distant edge of Valoria. Before, the land between had been flat and empty with nothing but dead grass.

Now, thick roots in the same chaotic mass of twists and turns that made up the wall of wood that created the border of the forest snaked across the grass and into the road, where what was left of it had been scattered for as far as his eye could see.

"She could not stop them," Enlin said aloud and swung back up onto his horse. How far ahead were they? Had the army already breached the walls? He looked to the edge of the Silvanna Woods. Some of the thinner trees lay broken, the ground trampled, and small branches crushed.

"Prince?" Rylan asked.

"The army hid within Silvanna and waited for us to pass. They are far ahead of us."

The Grandmaster motioned with his arm and without hesitation, the Knights moved to obey, determination mixing with a thirst for battle. Enlin had noticed the gleam spring to life after the news that Vyell had been breached had been brought.

As he urged his horse to speed, he felt an answering birth flare to life within him. He had failed to protect his Kingdom, but he would not allow them to take the victory.

The walls of his Kingdom were in view when the shout carried back. His stallion labored to breathe as it answered his cue to stop. Enlin rode forward to take his place at the head.

Bodies littered the ground. The scent of burning wood did not need the black smoke to tell him the battle was inside the walls. Men fought at the gates, and it was there that Enlin's eyes were drawn.

The shadows that engaged his own soldiers were peculiar. "What are they?" a man near him questioned, his voice thick with fear.

"The Fallen," Enlin answered. He pressed his heel into the

sides of his tired horse and rode out before his men, cantering along the ranks. "On this day, you will fight for your Kingdom! For your families and for those that will come after! Every one of you has trained for this! Do not fight with your eyes, but with your heart!"

Pulling his sword, Enlin turned his horse to face the battle in play. He heard the answering ring of metal being drawn.

The Grandmaster rode out, secure in his ability to lead. Enlin knew this was not his first war. "Take back the gates!" Garin shouted and his men lifted their voices in a loud roar that reminded him of a phrase his grandfather had liked to say; "When the Lion roars, he leads with his intent."

CHAPTER 24

*H*is advice to his men had been as much for him as it had been for them. Enlin's first close glimpse of one of the Fallen was startling. It was a man, but it also was not. The eyes were fully black, lash-less, and the skin split from the outer corners into the hairline, gaping red without blood.

The naked arms and chest lacked substance beneath the skin, and though the creature looked weak, when the sharpened, thin metal rod it held slashed toward him and met his sword, he could feel strength.

Its legs were muscled and powerful, its feet quick and nimble as it sprang toward him. 'Unbound' came to mind as Enlin met its next furious swing.

"Do you fight for yourself or for Aviore?" he demanded as he parried. The creature did not answer as it continued its onslaught. Enlin's years of training in the yard served him well. He had challenged many a skillful Knight and won, but his skill was matched here. He did not dare glance to see how his men fared against the Fallen they fought.

The air was ripe with the sound of heavy breaths, the echo of steel, the cries of small victories, and occasionally the claim of death. Enlin knew when it was one of his own versus one of them. The screams that rose into the air before they faded away were piercing and chilling.

A second one came at him, and he barely managed to block the thrust that surged toward him. Using a move he had learned more for fun than as a defensive move, Enlin pushed hard off the ground and flipped back, pulling the dagger in his boot as he did.

Relying on the ability and instinct that only came from years of training, Enlin landed and used the shadows in the air to aim his sword and dagger. He felt the jolt along his arm when his sword met resistance, not from the rods the creatures used to fight, but from flesh.

Grimacing even as he refocused, he twisted his sword as he pushed it deep, his reward the scream that pierced his ears and skimmed a tremor over him even as he faced off with his second opponent.

There was no time to think of the life he had just ended. No time to grieve or wonder if there would be anyone else to mourn the loss. Enlin fought, using all his faculties, ignoring the pain when his arm was sliced, his thigh nicked.

More than one fell at his hand. He gained the open castle gate, fought beside his Knights as they took on the hordes of Fallen that waited inside. It was not just his Knights that raised their swords beside him. A face he recognized from the market resolutely joined him, a metal rod in both hands.

Together, they felled more of the creatures. The man fought as valiantly as one of his Knights, and with just as much skill.

Exhausted, blood that was his own and blood that was not staining his skin, Enlin was glad to take a moment to breathe when they found themselves unengaged. A glance around showed several of his Knights taking the same opportunity, and too many bodies to count lying in more blood.

Not just the Fallen. There were Knights, soldiers, peasants, and even a few women. Rising, Enlin searched for anyone that needed aid, noticing as he did so that the Fallen all seemed to have the same types of marks upon their backs. Red lines split the skin but were not bloody. There were different formations and numbers of the strange red scars, but all appeared to have them.

"Do you know where the Princesses are?" he asked the man who had fought with him.

"I'm sorry, Your Highness, I do not. I have been fighting since they broke through the gate."

Several Knights had joined them. Some from the company he had brought back with him, and a few from the Knight Order that had been left behind to defend the Kingdom.

"Where is the Royal family?" he asked one.

Again, he was not given the answer he sought. "Felix!" Enlin called to one of the Valor Knights. "Secure the grounds and see to the wounded. Be ready for another onslaught. This is not over. Silver Knights, with me!"

All obeyed. Garin, his sword glistening red, called out orders as they entered the castle. Enlin was not surprised to find Viker and many from the invading army in the throne room.

Viker was seated on his father's throne. The King was bound, gagged and on his knees before the enemy. Enlin was relieved to see his father still lived. The eyes so like his own that found his were full of defeat and sorrow.

He could see no sign of any of the Princesses. Telphee was being held loosely by men Enlin assumed were from Aviore. There was only one of the Fallen in the room. Had his men managed to kill the rest, or had a different agenda drawn them elsewhere?

"Ahh, the Prince has arrived," Viker greeted him, his tone and manner mocking.

It was difficult to tell who had the advantage by number in the room. The two swords aimed at his father gave the power to Viker.

"What do you want, Viker?" Enlin hesitated to lower his sword. He could not allow himself to be taken captive as well.

Viker leaned forward, his eyes angry and full of hatred. "My daughter." He spat the last word accusingly.

The word slammed into Enlin, nearly felling him. He locked his knees and tightened his grip on the sword that had faltered in his hand. Breeon was his daughter? Denial surged. Questions formed. Betrayal was foul in his soul.

She had brought war after all. Alayna had been wrong.

The implication was too much. "Did she know?" he stuttered. He was bound to her. Struggling to gather his thoughts to clear the web that clung sticky and messy in his mind, he tried to decipher what this meant.

A marriage was meant to align Kingdoms, not tear them apart. What purpose had Viker hoped to gain by sending her as his pawn? The throne he perched on haughtily could not be his without the death of the King. Without Enlin's own death.

Clenching his teeth and burying the pain weaving around his heart, Enlin shifted his sword slightly and shot a glance at both Rylan and Garin. There would be no choice but to fight, even if it meant the loss of his father. They could not allow the Kingdom to fall into Viker's hands. His father would know that.

"Her allegiance belongs to me," Viker answered. "That is why I am here. I have come to claim what is rightfully mine."

From the corner of his eye, Enlin took in the subtle shifting of stance and sword. His men were ready. "You could have done this another way. We could have become allies. What purpose is there in senseless murder and the loss of peace?"

"There can be no peace!" Viker shouted. His hands shook where they rested on the throne, his fingers curling into fists. "I will have my revenge. I will see your father suffer as I have suffered. He will feel pain and loss and wallow in his regret."

Something made no sense. Never once had he heard the King even mention the name. What connection could they have? Enlin glanced between the two. They seemed close to the same age. Had they known each other in the past? His speculation would solve nothing. His father could not answer his questions. He gave his attention back to his adversary.

"Is there no resolution we can agree upon?"

A sneer twisted Viker's lips. "We can agree upon your torture. Would you prefer to have him watch you be torn apart by the Fage's, or chopped into pieces by a blade?"

"Neither!" Garin shouted and surged forward, his men taking his cue and doing the same to engage those nearest them.

There was no time to think about what a Fage was, how tired he was, or the places on his body that screamed in pain. Once again, his weapon clashed against another, his resolve challenged his opponent, and his passion for his people and Kingdom gave him the strength he needed to fight.

When finally, his blade met with nothing but air and he and his Knights stood over yet more bodies, it was Rylan that took the sword from Enlin's hand and sheathed it.

"Where is the King?" Enlin breathed out. He was dizzy, his throat dry.

"Gone," Garin answered, shoving his own sword home.

"Taken," Rylan corrected, gripping Enlin's arm. "They took him, Prince. He is still alive."

"And Telphee? Is he one of the dead?"

"We believe they took him as well. Come, we need to rest and take care of our wounds," Garin stated, moving in front of Enlin to capture his attention. "Where can we go that is safe?" Nodding, Enlin started toward the servant's entrance. He heard

Garin ordering Knights to gather supplies but did not stop. Using a hidden door, he led the way to the room he had taken Breeon to, refusing to think about her as he lit the torch and waited for the soldiers to enter.

"Elias, can you remember the path?" Given acknowledgement, Garin motioned for the Knight to go back before turning into the room himself and looking around. "Who knows this room is here, Prince?"

"The King, I'm sure. Other than that, I don't know. It has not been in use for years."

He was helped to an abandoned pallet in a corner. Knowing he could trust those surrounding him, Enlin closed his eyes and let the pain and exhaustion claim him.

The low murmur of voices woke him. Enlin turned his head, watching the cluster of Knights. A paper was spread between them. Terrick drew with a chunk of charcoal while Garin and Elias motioned with their hands over the paper.

Pulling in a deep breath, Enlin took stock of his body. There were a few places that hurt, more so with movement, but nothing that he felt would prohibit him from continuing.

He sat up slowly. Many men slept on makeshift pallets around the room. His thigh was bandaged, as was his arm. A Knight moved to his side. "Your Highness." A cup of water was held out.

"Thank you, Tyon." Enlin drank slowly, emptying the cup. Bread and cheese were held out next. "Where do we stand?" he questioned as he began to eat.

"Viker has few men, Your Highness, but we are unsure how many of the Fallen there are. As of yet, we have not located if there are large numbers hidden somewhere on the castle grounds. Nor have we found any sign of the Princesses."

"Nyala knows of many of these rooms," Enlin commented.

Tyon indicated the grouping of men around the paper. "We have been attempting to construct a map of the castle. Where we have searched, where we have not."

"The King?"

"We believe Viker has him secured in the King's chambers, Your Highness. More of the Fallen have joined their soldiers there. Also..."

"What is it, Tyon? Hold nothing back."

"If I hadn't seen it with my own eyes, I wouldn't believe it, Your Highness, but it seems these... creatures... have the ability to climb walls and jump great distances."

Rylan sat down beside him. "Your color is better, Prince. I was concerned." A hand settled on his shoulder. "Unless there are more of the Fallen, we believe we can obtain a victory."

"However," Garin said, stepping in front of the Prince. "It would be a great oversight on Viker's part to be so ill-prepared. We cannot trust such an easy victory."

"Easy?" Enlin countered bitterly, thinking of the dead strewn over the grasses and stone. Of Breeon's betrayal. The King on his knees before a man who carried a grudge for something unknown. What more had been lost?

"Forgive me, Your Highness, I meant only that wars are not won in a day." Garin knelt before his Prince, bowling his head.

Enlin sighed, rubbing at a sore spot on his neck. "What is our next move, Garin?"

Lifting his head, Garin answered. "The men have been nourished and now rest. When we are ready, we shall attempt to take back our King. I have men dispersed. Each one that returns brings valuable knowledge that we will use to take back what is ours."

Enlin nodded, glad for the man's intelligence and experience. He rose. "I can help with the map." Revealing the secret halls of the castle was not something he was fully comfortable with, but if it meant lives saved, he would choose to trust those he was giving the information to.

Every castle held its long-guarded mysteries. Giving them away was discouraged from birth. Not even Telphee with all his gained expertise knew of the hidden paths and rooms scattered throughout the castle.

Now, Enlin knew that the age of the castle was an advantage. Silvera was one of the oldest Kingdoms and the spreading stone walls were expansive. Each successive King had added his own stamp to the layout and customs, until they had become like no other entity. It was part of the reason his father had attracted so many allies to his side.

The people and monarchies had found the methods he had adopted appealing and many of them had instilled the veers from old customs into their own ways of life.

From strategies of war and peace to day-to-day operations within the Kingdom, Silvera had always looked for ways to benefit both higher and lower ranks. The friendships that had been formed from the alliances had proved to be favorable and gratifying to all participants.

Enlin wondered what could possibly have transpired between his father and Viker to cause such deep resentment and hatred. As he directed the layout of the map, he tried to work through the puzzle in his mind, examining motives in a search for resolution.

Elias returned, bowing quickly. "They search for something, Your Highness. Many rooms have been ransacked. It is not Viker that searches. It is the Fallen."

"What do they search for, Your Highness?" Garin asked. Enlin shook his head. "I don't know. Do you think they mean only to be destructive?" He directed the question to Elias, who shook his head.

"No, Your Highness. They are searching for places where things could be hidden. It is not mindful destruction."

"More secrets," Enlin muttered. "I tire of them."

"Your Highness?" Garin questioned.

Enlin sliced a hand through the air to indicate he would give no further explanation for his comment. "Have any of our scouts returned?"

Elias nodded. "Yes. Felix gathers their reports, Your Highness. Vyell sustained great loss and some places still burn, but they are no longer under attack. It was quick and it was brutal. Fage's scaled the wall, took out the guards and lowered the gates."

"Fage's?" Enlin interjected at the mention of the term again.

"The Fallen, Highness. That is what they are called." At Enlin's nod, Elias continued. "The Silvanna Woods suggests the army hid there. What I understand is a cabin you frequent has been torn apart, and the ground gives credence that their number is higher than we first thought. The Fage's far outnumber Viker's men."

"You know this by their footprints," Enlin stated. The Fage's wore no shoes upon their feet. Elias inclined his head in confirmation.

"The towns of Avarila and Rathven to the west are untouched, nor do we see any signs of their presence near the Illuvian Lake or the Riavon Mountains to the south."

This was good news. Nyala knew the land well. If the women had escaped, he knew Nya favored the caves within the Riavon. It was possible she could have gone there.

"What have you heard from the East territories?"

"Only that Valoria Woods does not show signs that they could have been or gone there. The scouts were too afraid to enter, so they tracked the perimeter. Other than what we passed along the road, nothing was disturbed."

That left only Vilitia and the town of Vynar on the south

side of the Athadon River. If the army had crossed, there were a few towns scattered along the banks to the Northeast, but the river marked the Eastern border of their Kingdom.

"The scouts we sent to the South will need more time to return, Your Highness," Garin commented.

The man was right. Once they had learned Vyell had been attacked, Garin had directed a scout be sent to every ally Kingdom to both warn them and be assured of their safety.

"Do we need to request more aid?" Enlin asked the Knight.

"Our army is still strong, Your Highness. Felix has stationed companies of our soldiers within the Kingdom, and they have been ordered to guard their region and hold to the death, if need be."

Enlin sincerely hoped there would be no need. "Do you have more to report Elias?"

He did not and Garin dismissed him. "Prince Enlin, with the King in such a precarious position, I recommend strongly that you stay hidden here while we secure your father."

"No," Enlin responded and stood. "I will fight with my men. Let me speak this now lest the need for it come to pass and the words are not spoken." He looked around, meeting each set of eyes momentarily.

"If this war claims the life of the King and my own, the throne shall fall to Kahlee. It is your duty and honor to pledge the same loyalty to her as you have to my father and to me. She will need guidance and strong men who will be proud to serve her as Queen."

Garin fell to a Knee and bowed low over it. "Your Highness, I shall serve this Kingdom and its Ruler until I die, no matter if it shall be King or Queen upon the throne."

"As shall I," rang out as one-by-one, the men took up the same stance as their Grandmaster. Rylan too pledged his allegiance.

Humbled, Enlin thanked them all before bidding them rise.

"I know that Vyell has formed an alliance with Treasha. Prince Lienn spoke to me of a betrothal. With Prince Gevin of Ovsia already married, it would be wise to seek a union between Princess Kahlee and Prince Alpin of Vilitia. She will need a strong leader at her side."

It was not pleasant to speak of the things that needed to happen in the event of his death. Enlin did not focus on his emotions but tried to think like a King caring for his Kingdom. There was a coldness to it, and he wondered if the need to look at the whole rather than a small part, for objectivity, had been what had contributed to the man his father had become.

With the business side of running a Kingdom done, they gathered around the map once more to finalize their next moves. Voices conversed over the paper spread between the men. Gone was the heat and apprehension that had been present in the Council meetings. Now, there was steel and a determination within the tones of the voices that united in agreement over what was to come.

Enlin allowed himself to wonder over the Princesses. Where had Kahlee and Nyala gone? Were they hidden safely away? Or had their lives already been lost, and he was too late to do anything for either of them?

Inevitably, thoughts of them led to thoughts of Breeon. The lines on the map blurred as his eyes narrowed and anger flowed. Viker's daughter. The connection would never have occurred to him. Had they sent a missive to Aviore questioning if they knew of her? He was not sure.

The directive had included the Kingdoms they knew little of. In truth, although Aviore had built a small castle and established borders, Kingdom Silvera had had little to do with them as their stature was not one of political significance.

Was that part of the reason for Viker's anger? Had Breeon been angry that she been ignored by those in the Kingdoms around them? Enlin found it difficult to believe time had gone by with none of the allied Kingdoms learning of one so beautiful as Breeon, of marriageable age. Many men were swayed by such a simple thing.

Another thought occurred to Enlin. "Has anyone knowledge of Viker? Does he have a royal lineage to claim the title of King in his own right?"

"Telphee would know the answer to that," Rylan answered.

"How did they take the King so quickly?" Enlin had been so consumed on ways to retrieve his father quickly that he had missed things that suddenly seemed vitally important.

"I asked the same question, Your Highness," Garin responded. "The Valor Knights assigned to him as guard have still not been found, and when the alarm sounded that we were under attack, the King was nowhere to be found. We thought he had been taken to safety until we came upon him in the throne room under Viker's control."

"And how did they manage to breach the castle gates within such a short span? We should have been able to hold the walls for weeks, at least." Something was amiss and Enlin's mind scrambled to find the detail that eluded him.

Priv, one of the Valor Knights, answered. "The Fage's, Your Highness. They scaled the walls with little trouble and were upon our guards in the towers before we knew what was happening."

"They came also from the West," Aurri, another of the Valor Knights added. "I had forgotten until now. I remember as I fought one of the Fallen that I saw a unit of men coming at us from the West, with no sign of a battle upon them. I had only a few seconds to think it odd."

"Someone let them in," Enlin stated, looking around at

the men. His hand curled into a fist on the map. Breeon. The betrayal continued its assault of his heart.

"Who would have done such a thing?" Garin questioned, his shock evident. If Enlin had not been wracked with the hurt the further layers of deception wrought, he might have applauded the man's lack of understanding for disloyalty.

Stepping back, Enlin checked first one gauntlet, and then the other to be sure they were secure. "Viker will give us the answers we need. Let us commence with this capture. I tire of having only a partial picture of the things that dare to try to divide my Kingdom. Today, we take it back."

CHAPTER 25

They entered the hidden hallways, splitting along the way to disperse men to as many entries near the King's chamber as possible. All the entrances and exits had some form of peephole to aid in secrecy, so without a concrete way to signal, each would determine their own course of action by what they saw.

Enlin heard the first scream of the Fallen before his unit of men had reached their destination. Knowing there would be no hiding the impending attack now, they increased the pace.

A cry from one of their own echoed as they spilled out to join the battle. The stone walls made the clang of metal-on-metal sharper. And the battle more dangerous. The Fage's used the walls to fight, jumping to the stone and crawling up to push off and spring at their prey. The agility gave them the advantage.

"Back-to-back!" Garin shouted and Enlin and the others obeyed, pressing in to create a circle that faced out. "Every other man, turn in!" Garin commanded, and it was done, creating a defense that gave them the eyes they needed to protect each other.

A Fage mounted the wall and jumped at the circle and met its end when a sword was raised to meet it.

Two others leapt at the circle, attempting to fell them. The rod it held hit the hard floor and jolted its body awkwardly, giving a Knight the opportunity to drive his blade into its side, raising another ear-splitting scream.

Muted shrieks from the dead told Enlin the King's chamber had been achieved. The beings they fought were fewer in number, but he knew there would be more guarding Viker and his father. Propelling himself forward, he slammed his sword into flesh, feeling the sickening thud he had come to recognize as metal hitting bone.

Ducking to miss the blow of a rod, he knocked a Fage down at the ankle and turned away to engage another as Rylan sank his sword into its chest.

A cold hand wrapped fingers around his neck from behind and pressed, the strength crushing his breath. Enlin struggled to obtain air, lurching his body forward in an attempt to free himself from the grasp. It did not loosen. A weight landed on his back, pushing him down. He thought he had met his end when abruptly he was able to suck in a breath and the weight was gone.

A strong hand wrapped around his arm to help him up. Garin's eyes met his for a moment before the man gave his attention back to the combat.

The stench of death was heavy. "There are shields on the walls in the King's chamber," Enlin said to Garin and Rylan as they entered the doorway. The information was passed along the line of men. His father's chosen method of decor would offer them more protection from the long reach of the Fage's.

The room had been torn to pieces. The shields were lying in ready access on the floor. Tapestries lay in shreds, the mouth of a lion open in a gaping roar shifting beneath

Enlin's feet as he lifted a shield and slid it into place upon his arm.

He caught a glimpse of his father as he engaged two of the Fallen and one of Viker's men. He was bound and bloodied, but alive. There was no sign of Telphee.

Enlin used the shield to meet the thrust of a rod, the force shoving the rod back through the hands gripping it and into the stomach of the Fage, who screamed its rage, but did not die.

Holding his position in the center of the room, knowing proximity to the walls mattered, he danced with his opponents, clinging to his focus as they came at him again and again.

Viker had chosen his guard well. The Fallen possessed more skill in battle than his own men, and those that were left fell quickly. Viker himself huddled near the King, walled off by a cluster of Fage's that stared with their unblinking black eyes at the grappling men that fought.

Enlin's muscles protested the overuse. Warm blood leaked down his leg from his reopened wound. His mouth was dry, his throat raw from the choking grip that had almost taken his last breath. He drove his sword deep into yet another of the enemy and braced himself for the next that did not come.

Breathing labored, Enlin readied for defense and swept the area around him. The only Fallen left were those that guarded Viker. He did not allow his eye to rest on the bodies of fallen soldiers. He gathered the faces of those that were left standing quickly, relieved to see Rylan's among them.

There were four Fage's and twelve of the Silvera. The enemy was positioned near a corner, giving the Fallen a weapon of stone.

Garin stepped into place beside him. "Four-by-four," he murmured. It was a strategy and the men hurried to obey. Four in front, four in the middle, and four at the back.

"This victory is ours," Garin stated from the frontline. He moved forward and in unison, so did the rest. Shields rose. Hands tightened on hilts.

Viker placed his dagger against the King's throat.

Garin stopped.

The King sighed, a long expulsion of defeat. His eyes met his

sons. "They want the feather," he breathed as a tear spilled from his eye. "Do not give it to them."

Garin took another step. Enlin sucked in a breath and roared in protest when the thin metal blade slid across his father's throat, teardrops of blood raining over the pale skin to soak the brocade shirt that bore the Lion emblem of Silvera.

The Fage's lifted as one to the walls. Garin shouted out commands. A scream rose, then another and another, until the last died off into silence and Enlin turned to face the enemy he wanted to take on.

Elias held Viker and shook his head as his Prince advanced. "We need him alive."

"Your King lies dead at your feet, and you wish for him to live?" Enlin spat.

"This battle is not yet won," Elias responded.

A hand fell upon Enlin's shoulder. "Elias is right." Rylan spoke softly at his side.

His hand shook as he lowered his sword to his side. The metal gleamed red. Blood soaked into the carpet beneath the tip of the blade. Enlin turned away to kneed at his father's side. Gently, he closed the lifeless eyes.

"Why did you move?" he choked out.

"We could not save him, Your... Majesty." The sorrow was there in the words Garin spoke. The title, directed both at the departed King and the new one was cloaked with regret.

"We need to secure the castle immediately." Garin, ever

the Grandmaster, did not let his grief diminish his role. He gave out his orders as Enlin mourned at his father's side.

Rylan was the one sent to draw him away. "The Princesses may still be in danger. It is time."

"Her lies have caused this," Enlin said bitterly as he stood.

"And she will be dealt with accordingly when we find her, Your Majesty," Garin promised.

Enlin shook his head. "Please don't call me that. Not yet."

Rylan guided Enlin toward the door. "It is who you are now," he said softly.

He did not feel like one. Grief-stricken, broken, betrayed. Those were words that described him. Not leader. Not King.

Breeon was now the Queen, Enlin realized as they made their way along the halls of the castle. A Queen who had looked into the eyes of his father and proclaimed his death, knowing it would come because of her. A traitor, like the Queen that had come before her.

CHAPTER 26

*N*o resistance met them as they gathered the bodies of their soldiers and people.

Garin assembled his army before the castle walls and took stock of those that remained. Those injured were attended to.

The Priest prepared the dead for burial and attempted to offer comfort to those in mourning. The news that the King had been lost was held back to allow both Enlin and the Knights to maintain control.

Enlin questioned his trust of the neighboring Kingdoms. Losing a King had been ample enough reason for war in the past and they had already endured heavy losses. Nor did Garin believe they were done fighting. He had cautioned against lessening one's guard and the order had been given for vigilance.

Rylan accompanied Enlin to one of the suites reserved for lower ranks and pushed him to rest. Desperate to escape the barrage of emotion, Enlin was grateful for the darkness the drawn curtains provided and the sheltering screen of the blankets as he buried himself in the bed and closed his eyes.

Black eyes taunted him. Blood pooled. His father stared

up at him from dull green accusing irises. Breeon laughed mockingly.

His dreams were riddled with the assault of the trauma that had overtaken his life.

He refused food and drink when it came. Ordered any who sought his presence away. Commanded that the curtains stay closed. He cared not what happened outside of the walls. It was too hard to ponder his duty and the unknown. It was far easier to dwell in the shifting shadows of sleep and grief.

It was Rylan who dared to defy his gruff command to leave him be.

"I have given you all the time I can allow," Rylan countered firmly. "Your people need to see that you are well, and Viker waits."

Viker. Enlin thought of running his dagger over the man's throat and dispensing the same punishment on him the man had meted out for his father. But first, he wanted the truth.

Flinging the covers aside, he left the bed. He bathed in the waters Rylan had ordered prepared and dressed, deliberately choosing the tunic that matched the one his father had worn as he died, using his anger to fuel him through his motions.

"Tell me why I should not just slice your throat and be done with you," he demanded the moment Viker was brought before him.

A sneer twisted the shadowed face of the man. "It makes no difference. Your suffering has not come to an end."

Garin entered, followed by four men carrying a chair. It was set down and Viker placed into it. The chair was made of wood and the arms and legs opened, each with a circle for wrists or ankles. Once each of Viker's appendages were secured, a nail was driven through the wood on each side to immobilize them from movement.

Garin slowly walked up to stand in front of Viker. "You will answer the King's questions, or you will feel the wrath of

Silvera swiftly. I warn you I do not mean death." Garin turned sideways and gave Enlin a slight nod.

"How did you get the Fage's to join forces with you?" It was a question Enlin was more curious about than anything but seemed as good any to see if Viker would heed Garin's warning.

"Did you know your father was a cheat and a liar?" Viker jeered.

With barely a pause, Garin pulled the dagger at his side and took hold of one of Viker's fingers, slicing it off at the first knuckle. Viker screamed, his face contorting.

Enlin barely managed to contain his own. He steeled himself, wondering at the fault inside of him that made him want to cringe at the punishment inflicted on the man who had murdered his father in front of him.

"Answer the question," Garin demanded irritably.

Gasping as he struggled to contain his pain and trembling, Viker gave Garin a long look before he nodded his consent. Garin had proved that he would not show mercy.

"It was easy. I knew what they wanted, and I had only to dangle the bait to win them over."

"What bait?"

Viker set his jaw and Garin reached out.

"Okay, okay!" Viker shouted, the rest of his fingers curling inward. "An angel! I told them I could give them one!"

Garin scoffed. "That's delusional. Angels do not exist." Viker barked out a laugh. "Are you serious? What do you think the Fage's are?"

"An angel seems far-fetched," Garin shot back.

"They climb walls and jump like monkeys," Viker retorted. "Which seems more demon than angel," Garin argued.

"They're Fallen Angels!" This remark Garin had no response to. "Do they know you lied to them?" Enlin asked.

Viker narrowed his eyes, a sharpness gathering in the depths that Enlin did not like. "I did not lie. Once they have her, she will come."

"Who do you speak of?"

"My daughter, and her mother! I had heard you were smarter than you seem, King Enlin."

Enlin stared at Viker. Was the man saying the mother of his child was an angel? How could that be possible? Which meant, Breeon was... one of the Fallen. Viker was saying they were both Fallen.

Lurching to his feet, Enlin walked away from the scene before him. Breeon did not look like the Fallen. How did he explain the gold flecks he had seen in her topaz eyes? All the Fage's he had seen had blackened orbs.

And marks upon their backs. Stopping short, Enlin shouted as the image of the cold truth slammed into him. He turned to the closest wall and lifted fists, slamming the cupped ends of his hands into the tapestry that hung undisturbed and silent.

Yelling out his rage, Enlin pounded his fists again, feeling the jar in his wounded arm.

She had duped him so easily. They had taken her beauty and used her deceit and he had fallen for it. An apt description of who they were and what they did, it seemed. But, oh how it hurt. He hated to admit that he had begun to care for her. His heart had been betraying him as much as she had been.

All of it a lie.

"Enlin."

He leaned his forehead against the coarseness of the tapestry.

"Rylan, I can't take much more."

"Does your heart believe she conspired against you?"

"How can it not?" The sourness was there. He could not breathe or swallow without it consuming him.

"I don't believe it," Rylan stated.

Lifting his head and stepping away from the wall, Enlin faced his long-time friend. "She had the marks on her back that the Fage's all bore."

"What do you mean?"

He had thought her only hurt. "In the cabin. Those red slashes that look like cuts but are not. And she was bruised around them, as though they were fresh injuries. How can I discount that?"

Crossing his arms, Rylan studied him from over his nose. "How can you discount the obvious fact that she acts nothing like them? Her heart is obvious. She cares for people. I do not believe one can fake the innocence she carries with her."

"When did you become her advocate? She warned me! She predicted the fall of the Kingdom! She told me she could not marry me. She all but spelled it out for me, and I... I did not listen."

Rylan started back down the hall. "Walk with me. I am meeting with Garin for the daily report."

"Has anything changed?" Enlin wasn't sure he cared, but the question was prudent.

"Your sisters and Breeon are still missing. There is no sign of more Fallen. Reinforcements have come."

Enlin thought of Nyala and knew that he did care. He imagined her frightened and withdrawn and Kahlee making it worse with her sharp tongue and annoyance at Nyala's soft demeanor. "Do you think they are alive?"

"Yes, I do," Rylan said with confidence. "And I think your wife is the reason for it."

"Do not call her that," Enlin snapped through clenched teeth.

"We received word from one of the Valor that they were seen by some of the peasants retreating. Breeon fought off two of the Fage's to protect them."

Enlin cast about for why Breeon would have acted in such a way. "Part of the plot?"

"Your Majesty, you are not hearing me when I say I do not think the Queen is part of the plot."

"Don't call me that, and Viker has told us that she is."

"An unwilling pawn, then. Why else would she have protected your sisters and not handed them over?"

"I want to speak to the peasants who saw them fleeing."

Rylan nodded, lifting a hand as they stepped from the castle. A guard came forward to greet them, bowing before Enlin. "The Grandmaster is with the Armorer, Your Highness. It is good to see you well."

Enlin shoved his hair back and nodded, not bothering to stop. "What reinforcements?" he asked Rylan.

"Each of the towns has a provision of men who train as a precaution. The citizens have taken refuge within castle walls and the men have joined us in a show of support and loyalty."

Frowning at the explanation Rylan well knew that he already knew, Enlin looked around. "So, Weston is here."

"He is, yes," Rylan acknowledged. "As is his wife."

Horses were hurriedly being saddled as they approached the stable. Garin and a few of the other Silver Knights hurried toward it. Enlin and Rylan met them in front.

The Stable Master rushed out, bowing. "Your Highness! Do you wish for your horse as well?"

"Yes, and Rylan's." He faced Garin. "What is happening?"

"Movement near the base of the Riavon. One of the townspeople has just brought news." Garin pointed at a soldier. "Fetch armor and weapons for Rylan and the Prince immediately and send the rest of the Silver and Valor Knights here."

The soldier ran to obey. The Stable Master shouted for more horses to be saddled. Enlin entered the stable to help.

His anger burned and the thought of a fight gave him something to direct it toward.

The ensemble wasted no time mounting the readied horses and departing. A second assembly was ordered to be prepared and to follow in case they came upon the rest of the Fallen and found themselves engaged in another battle.

They cleared the southern edge of the castle, passed over the small stream that ran parallel to it, and skimmed under the budding Wisteria trees that his youngest sister adored.

The trees were scattered over the property leading to the Mountains. Their trailing tendrils were bare of color but did not lack substance. Beyond the grounds where they clustered, a clearing opened before the foundation of the mountains could be reached.

A small grouping moved slowly toward the castle. It was not the Fallen. Enlin recognized the dark glint of Kahlee's hair and the sheen of Nyala's. Between them, they supported a woman. At such a distance, Enlin did not recognize her. One of their Ladies-in-waiting if he could judge by her dress and the long, dark fall of her hair.

Spurring his horse, joy surged through Enlin at the sight of his sweet sister. And was quickly doused when a keening screech filled the air and Fage's erupted from a section of ground covered with boulders not far from his sisters.

Kahlee screamed and let go of who they held. Nyala did not. She bent, struggling to grapple with the woman. Running forward toward the soldiers coming to their aid, Kahlee left the other two behind, fear evident on her face.

Behind her, Enlin watched the unknown woman push herself up and the shock that tightened his body drew his horse up short. The woman was Breeon. She pulled the blades from her back and turned toward the Fallen, stumbling. A glint at Nyala's side revealed that she held a weapon as well.

Drawing his sword, Enlin bent low over his horse and

surged forward. He was unable to tell who would reach them first. It was obvious that Breeon was weak. Her attempt to stop the first of the Fallen that reached her was sloppy, but somehow, she managed to hold the Fage off. Nyala hovered behind her; the dagger held out in front of her as though it were her enemy. Tears glistened on her cheeks.

A Fage jumped, high over Breeon and landed behind Nyala, who gave a startled scream and turned, blade out even as she cowered low. Breeon shouted a protest and drove one of her short swords into the Fage she fought, shoving it away from her as she jerked her body around to push Nyala out of way to engage the other.

The Knights descended upon the creatures, joining the fight. Enlin held his aim toward his sister, watching Breeon fall as the rod her opponent held slammed into her blade.

He was almost there.

The Fage stood over Breeon, looking down on her. Enlin felt strangely detached from the speed of the activity around him as he viewed the creature bend down. It grasped at her shoulder and tore the fabric. Nyala yelled in protest and lunged at it.

"Nyala, no!" Enlin shouted.

The Fage lifted its head, and a sound came from its mouth that caused all the others to mimic the same sound. As one, they leapt away from where they were to land near Breeon.

Enlin reined in his horse and dismounted before it had time to fully stop. He sank his sword into the belly of the Fage that stood over Breeon, grabbing at his sister, and shoving her behind him as he did so.

"Stay down, Nya!" he ordered, swinging his sword in a wide arch at the other approaching Fallen. Horses swept in and Rylan shouted for Enlin, pointing at his sister once his attention was gained.

Nodding, Enlin continued to engage his enemy, feeling

the whir of air as Rylan's horse passed close and Nya's gasp as Rylan swept her up with him.

More Knights joined him, and they battled fiercely. The Fallen were driven in their pursuit, all of them attempting to grab at Breeon's prone body lying between the protective stance of the soldiers that fought them.

The second wave of soldiers arrived, enabling them to dispel with the rest of their attackers quickly. Only when he was sure that no Fage was left standing did Enlin turn his attention to Breeon.

He stared down at her. Gone was the golden hair and skin. She was so pale he could see the shadows of her veins. Her hair had darkened, and he could not help but stare at the mark beside her exposed shoulder blade.

Seeing it was what he needed to remind him he had been mistaken that she fought to save his sisters. He moved, reaching down to roll the body of one of the Fallen near her. The marks were there, unmistakably similar.

"What does that mean?" Garin asked.

"She is one of them," Enlin answered coldly.

"She was trying to save your sisters, not hurt them."

"No." No other word would formulate. The pain was a prickle that crawled over him, thousands of tiny stabs that penetrated deeply.

"Bring one of their bodies," Garin ordered, his soldier nodding and flinging one of the Fage's over the back of his horse. "I'll bring the woman," Garin said softly.

Enlin turned his back. He wanted to crawl back into his bed and never get back out.

CHAPTER 27

"*E*nlin!" Nyala ran to him, throwing her arms around his sides and holding him tightly as she pressed her cheek into his chest. "I was so afraid!"

Returning the hold, Enlin closed his eyes, relief that his sister was safe flowing through him. "I wasn't sure you were alive, Nya."

She lifted her face, tears gathered below her eyelids. "We wouldn't be if it weren't for Breeon. Two of them attacked us when we were trying to get away, but she killed them."

"You're safe now," Enlin soothed, not wanting to add to her distress by sharing any of his concerns about Breeon.

"We thought we were safe. Kahlee and I argued about leaving, but we didn't have any food or supplies, and Breeon was getting worse."

He hated that a part of him wanted to know more. "Did she sustain an injury during the attack?"

"No. I was with her when it began, Enlin. She was fine and then suddenly, she gasped, and I could tell she was in pain." Nya brushed away the tears that were falling now. "I asked her what was wrong, and she told me we had to find somewhere safe to hide."

"Why did you not go to one of the secret rooms, Nya? We searched them all looking for you."

"We were outside. Kahlee was only with us because she was bored."

"In your gardens," Enlin guessed. Before the Wisteria trees began, a large garden had been created for Nya. She spent time there every day.

"Yes. So, it seemed safer to go straight to the mountains. I knew of many caves there and thought we would be safe."

Curving an arm around Nya's shoulder, Enlin turned toward the kitchens. He had been told he would find his sisters there. Nya had obviously been watching for him.

"So, she knew they were coming." Which meant her job had been to keep his sisters safe. That made sense. Tucking them away until their use could be determined was a good war strategy. If Breeon had not gotten sick, he was sure a plan had been in place that had not had a chance to play out.

"She said they were crushing her. I did not know what she meant, but she could barely stand. I don't know how she found the strength to fight them off. It wasn't long we fled from the two she killed that even from where we were, we could hear the battle from the mouth of the cave."

"Nya," Enlin scolded. "You should have buried yourselves deep in that cave and stayed away from the entrance."

Resting her cheek against his arm, they entered the kitchens. Kahlee sat at one of the long wooden tables, eating a bowl of stew. Enlin went to her, pressing a kiss to the top of her head. "Kahlee, I am happy you are well."

"Breeon's not. What did they want from her?"

Taking a bowl of stew one of the kitchen maids brought, Enlin set it before Nya and sat beside her. "What do you mean, Kahlee?"

"Those things were after her."

"After Breeon?"

Kahlee dropped her spoon into her bowl and frowned at him.

"Yes."

"I wasn't aware you were an advocate of Breeon's."

Taking a chunk of bread from a tray, Kahlee tore a piece off

and dipped it into her stew. "She gets far too much attention, but if it wasn't for her, those things would have killed us and taken her."

"Did they want her so they could use her against us, Enlin?" Nya asked.

"They were not here for her; she is one of them."

Nya blinked at him, confusion wrinkling her forehead. She began shaking her head, slowly at first, then faster. "No, Enlin, that is not true!" she exclaimed adamantly.

"I agree, brother," Kahlee said, arching her brows at him. "Breeon is not one of those... whatever they are."

Enlin stood. "I tire of deception!" he exploded as he strode from the room. There was one person who had the answers he needed.

"Rylan!" he shouted in the hallway. "Rylan!"

"I will get him for you, Your Highness," a nearby soldier promised with a fast bow before hurrying away.

Enlin started toward the hall that would take him to his suite. If Breeon was being cared for, her room was the most likely place she would have been taken.

He did not bother to knock. The servants in the room startled as he burst in, dropping into curtsies. One rose from the bedside and rushed toward him, hushing him. "Forgive me, Your Highness, but the Princess sleeps!"

Enlin recognized her as Velynn. He remembered that Breeon had said the girl was kind to her. He could see loyalty in the fierceness of her protest at his intrusion, despite her disrespect.

"Has she awakened at all?"

A Lady-in-waiting stepped forward and pulled roughly at Velynn's arm. "Step back, girl! You should be flogged for speaking so to the Prince!" The woman dipped into a perfect curtsy.

Enlin recognized her as one of Vilitia's noble wives.

"She is dying, Your Highness. The Royal Physicians have come, and none can find reason for her malady."

They let him pass and Enlin stood over his wife, staring down at the paleness of her skin, once smooth and tinged with health. Now, veins were visible at her temples, along her hairline, and her neck. Darkness smudged hollows beneath her eyes and her lips, once so tantalizing in the moment he had allowed himself to wonder what it would be like to kiss her, were nearly as pale as her face.

She lay on her side facing him. Enlin hesitated only a moment before leaning down to loosen the ties at her neck and carefully slide the fabric from her shoulder to bare her shoulder. The mark was there, an angry bruise that had spread, with the snaking lines of red drawn like branched lines through the black.

Velynn hovered at his side as he put Breeon's gown back in place. "They thought those creatures had scratched her, but the skin is not split at all. I told them she had the marks when she arrived. Should I not have done that, Your Highness?"

Turning away from the bed, Enlin swept his eyes over the congregated women. "Leave us," he ordered. He reached out to take hold of Velynn's arm. "You stay."

He did not miss a look of jealousy from one of the servant girls toward Velynn, nor the haughty lifts of chin from the Ladies. Whispers reached him before the door closed behind the last. Enlin did not care.

"Velynn, you have served at the Princesses side since she arrived?"

Velynn nodded, smoothing the covers over Breeon. "She speaks to me as though I am her equal. She sees me when no one else does. She smiles at me as though I matter." Velynn clasped her hands in front of her and stood straight to meet his eyes.

"I was not with her, Your Highness, when the attack came. But I have heard the Ladies-in-waiting that were speaking of it. They left them to save themselves." Anger crossed her face, and she unclamped her hands to wring them in front of her. "I would not have left her!" she finished fervently.

"Velynn, has she ever said anything that would lead you to believe she meant this Kingdom harm in any way?" He held up a hand before she could speak. "Please, do not answer out of loyalty, but from truth."

She did not hesitate. "The Princess is not capable of such a thing! She would never betray you! Forgive me for being so pointed, Your Highness, but there was a look in her eye when she spoke of you."

Not words he wanted to hear. He was doing his best to bury every favorable emotion that rose regarding his bride. There was too much evidence of her deceit.

"That does not answer my question, Velynn."

Something soft brushed against his fingers. Enlin glanced down, his attention shifting quickly when he realized it was Breeon. Her skin was warm, which startled him. He remembered the coldness of the Fallen when he had come into contact with them.

"Princess!" Velynn leaned down before he could, reaching out to touch the back of her hand gently against Breeon's forehead. Enlin gently urged her aside and knelt, so his face was level

with Breeon's. Her eyes were partially open, bright with pain. "Did you start this war, Breeon? Do not lie to me."

She swallowed, the act taking her several tries. Her

eyelids drooped and pressed back open. "Feather." The word was barely audible, and he had to bend close. "Ny..."

"Ny? Nyala?" Why would Breeon speak of his sister? "They are safe. Both Nyala and Kahlee."

Her head shifted slightly, and a soft breath of pain escaped her mouth. "Ny..." Her attempt to swallow again took more than one try. "Not... safe."

"Nyala is not safe? Is that what you are saying?"

Her eyes closed.

"Breeon." He pressed a hand against her arm. "Breeon, please answer me!"

A soft flutter of her lashes. "Ny..."

This time she did not reopen her eyes. Velynn begged him to leave her be. "Let her rest, Your Highness. I will do my best to question her when she wakes again. I will not leave her side!"

Frustrated, Enlin rose. He believed the girl.

And if he chose to believe Breeon, his sister Nyala was not safe, and he had no idea why.

"Where is Rylan?"

CHAPTER 28

There was no sign of the soldier who had gone for him. Enlin had expected him to be waiting outside of Breeon's room, but there had been nothing but guards and the women he had dismissed.

Shaking his head, he ignored the scramble for answers and turned back into the kitchens. His sisters were no longer there.

"Where is Princess Nyala?" he inquired of the same soldiers. Again, blank looks. He waved at two of the men. "Find the Princess and bring her to me. Now."

Leaving the castle, he sought out Garin. "Where is Rylan?"

"With Telphee, Your... Highness."

Enlin slanted a look at the Grandmaster for his near slip.

"This is a new development. Where exactly was Telphee found?" "Stumbling from the rocks. He says the Fallen were holding him

there, but abandoned him in favor of going after your sisters.

He's a bit bruised and bloody, but he will live."

"So, they took him thinking he might prove valuable."

Enlin watched a couple of soldiers training in the yard. Garin had been running drills when he had found him.

"That is what he said, Your Highness. Rylan has been with him asking questions."

"We're missing something, Garin. Something important."

A shout of triumph rose from the spectators in the yard. One of the men lay on his back, his sword gone from his hand. Enlin rubbed both hands over his face. "Garin, it has been suggested that Nyala is in danger. I want Silver Knights with her at all times."

"Who told you this?"

"My wife," Enlin hissed, the anger rising to spill into his voice. Inclining his head back toward the castle, he headed back to meet his sister. Garin fell into step beside him.

"We need to search the grounds. There could be more groups of the Fallen waiting. It also might be pertinent to question Viker again."

"Ahead of you on the grounds search, Your Highness. I will wait for you to deal with Viker again. He needs to see that you are holding your own. You get anything else from your lovely bride?"

"No."

Nya was being led toward them. Enlin was sorry to see that she looked afraid. He pulled her into an embrace. "We're going to need to make sure guards are with you at all times," he murmured. "Why?"

"We are being cautious."

Nya smoothed a panel of lace on her skirt. "You did not send for Kahlee."

It was an astute observation. "Come with me, Nya," Enlin said softly. He took her to the room where the Council met, motioned for her to sit. Garin posted guards at the door and closed them in, standing in front of the window that looked out over the castle gates.

Enlin shifted a chair to face his sister and sat, taking one of her hands. He ran his finger over the smooth skin. She was far too young for this. Too innocent. He lifted the cuff of lace at her wrist, studying an abrasion that it just barely hid.

"I fell," she whispered.

"Nya, the King is dead." He could think of no other way to tell her.

He lifted his eyes, watched the horror and grief take over her. She shook her head in denial, sobs escaping, tears falling freely. Enlin licked dry lips, shoving down his own rise of emotion. "Viker from the Kingdom of Aviore murdered him. He brought this war. Breeon is his daughter."

She shook her head again. "No, En, that cannot be true!" A tear splashed on his hand. With her free hand, Nya pulled a cloth from her pocket and pressed it to her face.

"He told the Fallen an angel was here. He bargained with them. His daughter in exchange for the angel."

"So, they aren't gone," Nya said through her tears.

"We don't believe so. We have Viker."

"Then why is it not over?"

"It's war," Garin said from the window. "Planning, strategy,

pawns, possible scenarios. A spectrum of how to handle what if's that might or might not happen." He left the window to stand beside them. "They prepared for this, Princess Nyala. With Viker in our control, their end game has become all there is."

Enlin felt a prickle wash over him. He shot back in his chair, horror filling him. A knock sounded at the door as he stood and took hold of Garin's arm. "They believe Nyala is the angel!"

Rylan came in just then, assessed them. "Has something happened?"

Enlin repeated his conclusion.

"I was just about to tell the..." Garin glanced at Nyala, then back at Enlin. "The Prince, that such a notion is ridiculous and makes no sense."

"Garin." Enlin rose. "We need to speak privately."

He brushed a hand over Nya's soft curls. "I'm sorry that I have to leave you after telling you such a thing. Is there someone I can get to stay with you?"

Enlin knew there was not. If she had to choose anyone, it would be him. He wished he could change that for her.

"I want to be with Breeon."

"What? Nya!" He bent, grasping her shoulders. "Did you not hear what I told you? She is his daughter! She was a part of this!"

Nya shook her head, a fresh stream of tears spilling. "No, she wasn't, En. She wasn't!"

Spitting out his breath, Enlin paced away.

"Come along, Princess," Garin directed and helped her from the chair. "Give me a moment to see to her, Prince Enlin." He turned to Rylan. "Will I need to hear anything you have to say?"

"From Telphee? No. He had nothing helpful to offer." Garin nodded. "I'll be back."

Enlin watched Garin lead his sister from the room, a comforting hand around her shoulders. Garin was old enough to be her father and he wondered if it would be helpful for her to have a father figure at her side as she dealt with the grief he had given to her.

"Telphee is all right?"

Rylan gave his affirmation. "Shaken up, but nothing that won't heal. He, of course, wants to push for a coronation immediately and make a statement to the surrounding Kingdoms. Despite the ordeal, he was all business as is typical of Phee."

"Maybe you shouldn't have told him. You know he tends to not hold his tongue." It was too soon to change the focus from the threat still over his Kingdom. Right now, they didn't need a King, they needed to know they were safe. There was time to cling to the pretense of the King being kept hidden away for safety.

"Anger is not a good emotion to hold on to, Prince. It will cloud your judgment."

"She betrayed me, Rylan."

Rylan gave a short laugh. "She hurt you."

"You know it's more complicated than that!"

"I know Breeon is dying. The problem will take care of itself." Enlin had to turn his back. He didn't want Rylan to see the churning inside of him. Rylan was the closest thing he friend. He was the one he turned to when he needed to clear his mind. Except this time, he wasn't sure how to conflict had to a talk. To say it, how to voice the play of belief and disbelief that swung like a pendulum. Rylan was right. His emotion was clouding his judgment. It was just far more than anger.

A knock announced Garin's return. Servants followed him in with trays of food and drink. Enlin helped himself to some ale.

They were quiet after the servants had gone while they filled their plates. Enlin took a few bites before he spoke, telling Garin about the feather his father had spoken of, and the alleged darkness attached to the event.

Garin listened quietly until Enlin had finished. Stabbing a chunk of ham with his knife he raised it but ran his tongue over his teeth instead of eating it. "So, you both are saying..." He pointed the knife at each of them. "You actually believe in the existence of angels? Have you seen this alleged feather?"

"No," Enlin admitted.

Garin arched a questioning brow at Rylan, who gave a negative shake of his head.

"So, it could be a lie."

Rylan plucked a winter berry from the tray. "One could argue if the Fallen exist, why wouldn't others like them as well? There are many mysteries in this land we inhabit we know nothing about."

"That's what they were looking for," Enlin stated. "The Fallen. They wanted the feather," he added at their blank looks.

He tossed his knife on his plate and shoved it aside. "Would it be just as good as an angel itself? If we give it to them, they will stop pursuing Nya."

"No," Garin argued, leaning forward. "They will not. We could not take such a chance! We have no idea what they hope to gain with either your sister, if you are right, or with the feather."

Shoving back from the table, Enlin abandoned his chair. "I know who will."

CHAPTER 29

The Woods of Valoria were as ominous and intimidating as they had been the first time Enlin and his men had approached. Once again, he, Rylan and Weston dismounted their horses to begin moving through the maze of roots twining in arches and spirals over the forest floor.

It was deeper within the cover of the trees they noticed the difference. The colors seemed not as bright, the air not as fresh, the mysterious aura of darkness shrouded along the perimeter bleeding in to pollute the rest.

The brilliant sunset of leaves had fallen and lay shriveled over the path that widened that had first led them to Alayna.

"The Fallen could be in here, but I have seen no hint of them," Rylan commented.

Enlin, too, had kept his eye roving, his caution heightened for the same reason Rylan spoke of. Weston had been told every detail of the events that had occurred since they had last spoken. He knew Breeon lay dying, of her deceit, and of the hidden feather and the threat over Nyala.

They had not gone far down the path before Alayna

herself appeared, walking toward them along the center of the rustling leaves. She carried a bag at her side.

She spoke first when they met her on the path. "I will come with you." Her blue eyes looked less like the sky and more like the waters of the lake.

"Do you know what has happened?" Enlin asked her.

She moved and spoke as though a web covered her and hindered her every attempt. It was slight, but he noticed the peculiar sluggishness.

"There is no other choice now," she murmured in answer, and they turned to retrace their steps. Weston took her bag, hanging it from his horses' side.

"I have more questions," Enlin said as they walked.

"They will be answered soon enough," was her response and she gave him no more.

Rylan offered to have her ride with him beyond the forest, with a sidelong glance at Enlin that suggested he feared for his safety in her presence.

Enlin did not fear Alayna. She harbored more secrets, but none that he believed meant him harm.

"She is dying," Alayna said as they entered the gates. Her eyes sought Enlin's, and she searched his face. "You care," she stated.

Setting his jaw, Enlin looked away. "She has betrayed my Kingdom."

Alayna closed her eyes and spread her arms to her side, tipping her head back. Rylan shifted to allow her space for the movement.

"The Angel's Song,
ever does it rise.
The heart and soul given over
as I lift His glorious cry."

"What is she doing?" Weston questioned from his horse. "Lady, you're making a spectacle of yourself."

Enlin could not answer. From deep within him, a melody struggled to life, familiar but elusive.

"I call upon your power
and ask for favor from Your Hand,
hear my plea oh Majesty,
as I beg for healing of this land."

Alayna faltered suddenly, her arms dropping, eyes opening, and her head snapping down to fix on the castle ahead of them. "They wait in the shadows. She cannot hear me."

"Is clarity a word you know?" Enlin demanded.

"Ahh, there is my pretty wife," Weston exclaimed, a smile stretching over his face. He nudged his horse to canter forward, swinging down near the castle entrance to embrace her.

Enlin ignored their soft murmurs. He swung down and allowed the waiting stablehand to take his horse. Garin was coming out of the castle doors, his face pale, shock evident.

Frowning, Enlin started forward before realizing Garin's eyes were fixed on something. He followed Garin's gaze straight to Alayna. Curious, he watched the two stare at each other, tapping Rylan's arm.

Together, they watched them. Garin was the one who crossed the distance to stand in front of Alayna, but he said nothing.

"Maybe some privacy for this," Rylan muttered, nodding at some townspeople gaping at Alayna.

Agreeing, Enlin motioned for Weston to accompany them. Enlin took hold of Garin's arm and Rylan placed a hand at Alayna's elbow to guide her along. Seeking the shelter of the Council room, Enlin closed them in and took a seat to observe.

Weston appeared unconcerned, but his wife was obviously interested. Despite leading her away, her eyes were glued to the pair who had still not exchanged a word.

It made sense that the two knew each other, he supposed.

Garin had begun his training as a Knight in boyhood, and Enlin knew he had fought for his grandfather. The two had probably seen plenty of each other in the castle when Alayna had served the Queen.

To what degree had suddenly become the question. Unsure if either of them meant to speak at all, Enlin decided he would seek his answers. He cleared his throat. "Alayna..."

She jolted and swung her head to look at him.

"I have questions for you. Will you sit?"

She hesitated, casting a glance at Garin, but she complied as he had expected she would, gripping the table and lowering herself into a chair as though the movement hurt.

"The Fallen are after the feather, and Breeon believes my sister as well. However, that makes no..."

"Which sister?" Alayna demanded, interrupting him.

"Uh... Nyala."

Alayna lurched to her feet, tilting a bit before she righted herself, fear filling her eyes. "Where is she? We must go to her now!" She was already moving to the door, panic adding a slight tremble to her words.

"Alayna." Enlin stopped her with the firm command. "None of us will leave this room until you explain your reaction. You agree that she is in danger?"

"Yes! Is she alone? Did you see them go after her? Why do you

think she may be at risk? Please, can we find her while you tell me?"

Standing slowly, Enlin studied the woman before him. Tears had gathered in her eyes. The tremble had overtaken her body. "What do you know?"

"I'm more worried about what they know. If they have discovered who..." She bit down on her lip, her eyes shooting quickly to Garin.

"Alayna," Enlin commanded again. "I will not ask again."

Her eyes closed. She stilled for several moments, the

trembling stopped, and when he could see the blue of her irises again, there was a resignation there.

"They want her because of me, Your Majesty. Nyala is my... she is my daughter."

Shock did not seem an ample enough word to describe the sweeping plunge his emotions took before spiraling back up to overwhelm him. "You? But how? You were banished. How? You?"

"How did you know to call him Your Majesty?" Rylan broke in.

"I was shown the passing of the King. I knew that Enlin was coming for me. I know things."

"And now would be a really good time to tell me the real story, Alayna. The complete story."

She hesitated but sighed and moved back to the seat she had vacated, sinking into it heavily.

"My story is one that begins a very long time ago. I was sent here for a purpose; one I failed to fulfill. I have since sought redemption, but I am still suffering for my sins." She sought Garin with her eyes again for a moment before continuing.

"After your birth, Majesty, I did what I could to keep you safe. The Queen made numerous attempts to end your life and I was afraid she would succeed. Your father was not content with one son; he wanted assurance only more than one heir can provide. He spoke of this to me many times."

"When you were his mistress," Enlin supplied with an arched brow.

"You do not defy a King, Your Majesty. It often results in death." She gave him a pointed look.

Enlin could not argue. He was not sure his father would have chosen such a route, but death or imprisonment both took what one called life.

"I convinced myself I was doing the right thing when I persuaded the Queen to deceive the King and use a surrogate to gain his favor, without his knowledge. Kahlee was born, not a son. The Queen was angry, but then she became quite taken with the child for a time."

"Who are Kahlee's parents?" Enlin prodded.

Alayna gave him a negative gesture with her head. "A noble passing through had a short affair with one of the Ladies attending to your mother at the time. Forgive me, Your Majesty, but I suggest it is better for me to hold on to this secret."

"For now. Move on to Nyala."

"The Queen and I... never got along. She tolerated me, only because the King favored me, and she had no other choice. She knew what I was to your father, and I knew that she knew. When I conceived... I convinced her the child was the King's, but it was not..."

Enlin already knew how that had turned out. The child had been born, the Queen had died, and Alayna banished. "May I ask how two women, and my mother, managed to conceal such an often obvious... predicament for so long? And keep the truth from the King?"

"You will not like my answer."

"Answer it anyway," Enlin ordered.

She nodded her assent. "Your father... enjoyed his women. And tired of them quickly. I say this with no pride when I admit his infatuation with me lasted far longer than most. It was a fitting time when he decided he had finished with me. Your mother had done all she could to poison him against me and he shifted his attentions elsewhere. With a new woman capturing his eye and, in his bed, it was easy to hide myself away, and your mother demanded he leave her alone each time she was with child."

Weston's wife spoke up for the first time. "So, the King was... how do I say this delicately? The Queen and mistresses?"

"Yes," Alayna answered. "Wanting another heir, his only

other option was to do what he could to impregnate the Queen. Once she announced their efforts a success, he left her alone."

"You know the rest. After Nyala's birth, the Queen died, and I was banished."

"Who is the father?" Enlin asked.

Distress tightened her features. "Please do not make me answer at this moment."

"She's mine," Garin announced, but his gaze never left Alayna. He was tense, his arms crossed, shoulders tight, and eyebrows drawn in. Accusatory.

The admission was the last thing Enlin expected. And, apparently, Garin had not expected it either.

Garin was shaking his head, anger gathering in his eyes. "All this time..."

Standing, Enlin crossed to the window, staring down at the activity happening beyond the small room they occupied. Garin and Alayna would have to wait to discuss what had been done.

"Why does this make her important, Alayna? Her parentage?" Garin was a soldier. He was of the aristocracy and had once held lands, but he had no family and had given his whole life to the business of leading and training Knights for the Kingdom.

And Alayna lived alone in the middle of the woods.

"Your Highness... please look at me."

At her soft request, he did.

"You must understand what I say next must not leave this room.

I have harbored this secret closely for so long, and in the wrong hands..."

Enlin looked around. Rylan. Garin. Weston and his wife. He trusted them all. He lifted his brows when his eyes were on her again.

Her fingers twisted through each other, and her shoulders drew in. She swallowed, and tears slid down her cheeks, regret brutal in its rawness. "Once upon a time, I was an angel."

Would the unexpected never end? "Well," Enlin breathed out. After that, he did not know what to say.

"How does Viker play into all of this?" Rylan asked when the silence had stretched too long.

Enlin had been too wrapped up in Alayna's story to remember Viker. He was happy to let Rylan take over the line of questioning while he processed all that he had learned.

"Viker is but a pawn. I imagine the Fallen have been waiting for the right time and receiving the inquiry of Breeon's identity gave it to them."

"And my... wife? The one who betrayed both me and the Kingdom she claimed she would call her own once she became the future Queen? What of her role in all of this?"

Alayna stared hard at him. "You have imagined the worst of her and given her no grace. Have you heard the song?"

"What song? Do not begin the riddles again!"

"She is dying. Your last hope is the feather. Yet your faith has been too small. The Fallen have come to steal, kill, and destroy. And you allow it. Breeon is not your enemy."

"She is Viker's daughter!"

Alayna let out a laugh that started as a puff of air. "No. That is not the truth. Your heart knows the truth."

What did he do with that? How was he supposed to feel now? Did he believe her? "What is the truth then? Her memory loss? The marks on her back? How do you explain those? They are the same as what the Fage's bear on their bodies."

"The rest of your answers must come from Breeon. Please, take me to my daughter."

CHAPTER 30

"*A*re you unwell, Alayna?"

The stone halls echoed their steps. The odd sluggishness that had been present in Alayna's movements since she had first approached them in the woods seemed to be worsening.

"They are strong here..."

Rylan pulled his sword at her words. Garin too as he wrapped an arm around her waist. Enlin did not miss the strained mix of tenderness, concern, and anger in the gesture.

Weapons ready, they approached the kitchens. Garin had placed Nyala there under guard, with the added presence of the staff able to attend to her needs and keep an eye on her as well.

A smile brightened her face when they entered. Enlin sheathed his sword and accepted her into his arms. "I'm sorry I left you," he murmured.

"Can we go to Breeon now?" Nya tipped her head back, a plea in her eyes. "I worry so for her."

There were too many eyes and ears in the kitchens. He could all but feel the longing coming from Alayna to his side.

189

Wrapping an arm around her shoulders, he steered her into the hall. If Alayna spoke the truth, there was no danger in taking her to see Breeon. And, if the rest of the answers would only be gained from her, then he had a need to see her as well. Dealing with his emotions would have to wait for a time when the stakes were lower.

"There is more I must tell you, Nya. It will be as hard as the loss of the King."

"Is it because of her?" He followed her eyes to Alayna and nodded.

"She is sick like Breeon is," Nya whispered to him.

He could not get her words out of his head as they walked the halls to the suite that held his wife.

Enlin and Nya were in front when he heard Garin call Alayna's name. He turned in time to see the Knight catch her as she fell. Rylan, too, shot forward to help. The seconds his attention was diverted was too long. The coldness that pressed in against him was thick, Nyala's scream short.

There was at least a dozen of them, swift as they surrounded his sister and took her from him, pulling her back, their skeletal hands on her like vines as they slunk back to hover against the stone.

Their swords were useless. Black eyes stared at him. No emotion was there but he knew they challenged him. Going at them with swords drawn would place Nya in harm's way.

One way was open to the Fallen. The hall that led to the Royal suites, and Breeon. Other than the hidden hallways, no other escape route would be available for them.

Enlin could hear Weston telling his wife to leave them and to send help. Unwilling to take his eyes from the mass of Fage's before him, Enlin quietly inquired of Alayna.

Rylan relayed that Garin was seeing to her. "She has told him that though the Fage's have long not been angels themselves, their darkness is great, and in such a multitude she struggles to keep it from affecting her. Something about familiar recognizes familiar."

"Garin may remember the hallways," Enlin murmured just loud enough for Rylan to hear. "Have him take Alayna and Cora from here and lead his men as quickly as he can through them to meet us."

Boots on stone told him Rylan obeyed. The Fage's, using Nya as a shield, moved further down the hall. Enlin feared what would come. The odds were against them. If there were more waiting in the shadows...

"Weston!" Cora screamed behind him. Enlin shifted his body, his sword ready, his stance allowing him a view either way. A smaller number of Fage's had taken Cora and were attempting to claim Alayna. Garin was already engaged in a fight with one of them and Weston faced off with those holding his wife.

A pale hand wrapped around Cora's neck, the fingers pressing. She coughed and gasped, reaching up to pull at them, panic widening her eyes. With its other hand, the Fage pointed at Enlin.

Weston was taking a small knife from a hidden casing at his back beneath his shirt. Enlin knew his aim was sure. He had never won a match against his friend throwing a blade.

"Your Majesty, I will have you know that I will not betray you!" Weston declared. "I will fight for you, this Kingdom, and all those in it until my death. This day will not be the day it ends!"

A flick of the wrist and the blade flew, landing with incredible precision in the center of the Fage's forehead. The chilling scream of death whistled, the hand loosened, and Cora fell forward, dragging in air with ragged breaths while she crawled toward her husband.

Without hesitation, Weston ran to her, lifting her and pushing her behind him before jumping to help Garin in his battle.

Rylan had not left Enlin's side. He would not leave him vulnerable.

Giving his full attention back to the Fage's holding his sister, Enlin scrambled to think of how they could gain back Nya safely. There would be no time for reinforcements now. They were nearing the room where Breeon lay. Those attending her were women. He tried to remember the number of guards posted. They would aid them.

Another shriek sounded, and another. "They are less equipped without their metal rods," Rylan murmured. "The Fage's fall quickly."

"They are not unskilled," Enlin warned.

"No," Rylan agreed. "But as I watch, I see things I was unable to see while engaged in battle. They are frenzied and there is a madness to their movements that makes them sloppy. I can see training, but it is inhibited by whatever has taken over their minds."

"A valuable insight," Enlin uttered, looking at those before him with new eyes. Yes, he could see it now. He had never thought before how much the eye expressed. With nothing but the black orbs that blankly stared out at the world, it was their body language one had to watch.

The fingers that held his sister twitched, as did the bodies of them all, in inconsistent spasms. A head would tilt or jerk, a shoulder would lift several times in quick succession. An arm or knee would bend, then straighten.

"Your Majesty, do you want us to attack?" Weston spoke beside him, screams fading into silence in the background.

"Cora and Alayna stay with us," Garin announced. "It is too dangerous to send them alone, and it is too late for help." Enlin shared his observations with all in a low voice. "The guards will add to our number. We will wait until we hear them initiate." He could not see much beyond the Fallen so he watched for the stone arch that would tell him they were close.

When it did come into view, no shout of danger filled the air and the Fallen continued their unhindered escape past the closed door.

Had the Fage's prepared for this? Taken out the guards? Enlin saw no sign of blood or a fight. Or had the guards seen the coming mass and hidden themselves away in the room to protect themselves?

Garin went to the door, meeting Enlin's eyes as he pushed at the wood.

One of the Fage's hissed, and the snaps and jerks momentarily skittered over the group like it was a single felt emotion.

The door swung wide and Breeon stood there, as though she had been waiting for just that moment. The missing guards held her up, swords drawn, and at her back stood Velynn, waiting with a frightened but determined look on her face, and in her trembling hand, a dagger.

"Stay back, Breeon," Garin warned, but Breeon took no heed of his words and moved through the doorway with the guards' help, her eyes seeking Nyala's.

"We will give you the feather if you release the girl," she stated, and though Enlin could tell she was weak, her voice was steady and firm.

He did not dare tell her they did not know where the feather was.

A collective hiss pinged among the Fallen again in response.

Velynn shoved forward. "No, Princess! You will die!" She held out the arm with the dagger, the blade trembling as she pointed it at the mass of Fage's.

"Step back, girl," Garin ordered. "We shall offer them no deal... Princess," he directed toward Breeon.

"They want the feather, not Nyala. If they do not get it, they will kill her." Breeon took another step toward them, her skin the same shocking white of her shift. Her veins had become more prominent. Enlin walked to her, feeling the weight of his guilt press sharp in his gut as he took the place of one of the guards.

"I doubted your loyalty, Breeon. Viker said you were his daughter and I believed him. The missing pieces seemed to fit and I..." He had no more words that would excuse his traitorous heart. "I hold little hope you will forgive me."

Through her shift he could see the angry bruising over her shoulders, the dark red that spread in branched lines not only on her back, but over her arms and the delicate curve of her lower neck.

"Will you trust me now, Enlin?" she questioned, looking at him for the first time.

"Yes," he answered without hesitating. Despite the darkness that had flooded the beautiful topaz of her eyes and stolen their brightness, he knew that he would. He had always wanted to, he realized. Needed to. She had given him no cause to question where her own heart lay from the beginning. Her innocence had never been a lie. "My mind defied what my heart has told me from the beginning."

"I do forgive you," she promised. "Now, we must take back what is ours. Do not question the things that come next."

She turned her gaze to Alayna. "It is time," she said to her, and Alayna nodded and the two moved to meet each other, Cora helping Alayna and Enlin supporting Breeon.

"You will take care of her for me?" The words were a sorrowful plea. "Tell her the things I am not able to?"

"I will," Breeon promised as Alayna lifted her hands to place them on either side of Breeon's face.

Tears that had spilled over and clung to Alayna's cheeks shattered. It was the only word Enlin could think of to describe it. The sound of wind filled his ears, warmth erupted in the space around them and throughout his body, and he heard the words to the elusive song, loud and clear.

He was unsure if it was only in his head or if the melody filled the air.

"I am Yours to use at will,
I open up my spirit for you to fill.
Guide every breath you give
I breathe you in so You may live.
With Your mighty roar in my ears
I lift my life to You here.
Covered in Your grace and mercy
I claim the victory."

Enlin recognized Breeon's voice singing the song, though she did not speak a word. While the meaning of the words filled him, he was enveloped in an indescribable power that he knew had everything to do with the two women before him, and nothing to do with himself. Nor did he need them to tell him that if he had not been holding on to Breeon, he would not have felt any of it.

They were all but vessels, he realized as the words sank into him. Allowing themselves to be used for something greater if one chose. He remembered the tale from his childhood where a single angel had defeated an army and vanished.

Would he lose Breeon? He had finally grasped the truth Alayna had told him he had known in his heart. Breeon too, was an angel. Not one of the Fallen, not one lost as Alayna was, but one who had somehow been given to him to care for and perhaps one day, love.

Would it come to that, Enlin wondered? Would he be given the chance, or would she perish this day?

CHAPTER 31

*A*layna crumpled, the movement so sudden Enlin almost let go of Breeon. Garin rushed forward to gather her prone body into his arms.

Breeon was changed. Gone was the transparent skin, the darkened eyes and hair, the shock of veins and bruises. Instead, she glowed, her hair, eyes, and skin glittering with gold flecks.

"Velynn, my short swords, please," she requested, her eyes on the Fallen, who had begun to hiss and shriek while twitching uncontrollably.

"We do not need the feather; they will come for me now. Cora, go for the Knights, quickly. None will touch you. Garin, leave Alayna be. There is nothing you can do."

Velynn was back, pressing the swords into Breeon's hands. The moment she took one step forward, several of the Fallen jumped, a chaotic madness in the sounds emitting from their mouths, but with Breeon's forward trajectory came a pulse of light that struck them in a wave, knocking them all back.

Garin shouted his rage and advanced, Rylan and Weston

at his heels and Enlin bringing up the rear. "Protect your Queen!" he shouted.

Their madness united them and though they engaged the men who came at them, again and again they merged and went after Breeon. The single-minded pursuit made them dangerous. Enlin was relieved when the Knights came to add their strength.

Once again, he called out his order to protect Breeon at all costs.

A weight slammed into him from behind, knocking him to the stone floor, his sword slipping out of his grip to clang uselessly out of his reach. A hiss sounded near his ear, what clearly felt like a foot wrapped over the back of his neck, pushing his face into the stone.

Enlin attempted to roll, to fling the Fallen from his back and regain the advantage. Another weight covered his legs, the pressure against his neck eased and two shrill cries of death rose.

This time, when Enlin rolled, the weights slid off his body and he was able to grasp his sword and rise again.

"Swing left, Majesty," Rylan's voice called and Enlin responded, arching his blade, feeling the solid kick back as it met flesh before he had turned to meet his opponent.

"Their numbers diminish!" Garin called out.

"Hold!" Breeon answered, authority in her voice. "The last of them comes!"

Enlin was unsure of her meaning. He drove his sword home through the belly of a Fage and turned to the next, his quick glance down either side of the hall revealing no seeking throng of Fage's.

"Move to the East wall! They come from the window!" Breeon shouted.

Enlin did as she asked, having only seconds before shattering glass exploded in at them. He felt a sting of pain at his side and jaw. He had no time to consider how they had managed to gain the upper window before they poured through in hordes, the hisses, and spasms as violent as their immediate assault.

He lost sight of Breeon as his men surged forward in the onslaught. His side throbbed. The arm he used to hold his sword ached. His skin was sticky with blood, his own warm on his neck from the cut on his jaw.

Enlin saw Breeon when he crouched low and shifted to cut two Fage's off at the knees. She was pulling her own blades from the chests of two bodies lying on the stone.

He slammed a shoulder into a group of them that lurched at him, huddled close together. It was hard enough to throw them off balance and allow him to take a couple out of the equation.

Scream after scream echoed in the high hall. Enlin doubted he would ever forget the sound. It would haunt his dreams and memories.

Moving to find a section of stone not cluttered with bodies, Enlin saw one of his own men staring with sightless eyes up at him. He allowed himself a moment too long, a Fage leaping at him with a weapon in its hand.

Enlin fell back, lifting his sword in an attempt to protect himself. Thin metal coated with blood erupted from the Fage's stomach and a chill shriek of death hissed out.

His wife flashed him a smile as the body crumpled before she turned to take on another.

"They attacked me while I was admiring the brilliant colors of Valoria Woods," Breeon said, wiping blood on her already stained shift. The gesture left a garish streak on the white fabric.

"I was so caught up in the beauty of the curving wood and splashes of color spread out below me that I let down my guard."

Garin rolled the body of a Knight, pressing his hand against the neck to check for a pulse.

"There were three of them, and I imagine they had been waiting for just such a moment, as the attack was planned. While I engaged those three, two more came at me from behind and tore at my wings. I fought, but the pain was great, and they were relentless."

She wiped her other short sword clean and grasped both in the same hand, joining them as they checked those that had fallen while she told her story.

"As I fell, I heard an old, familiar song rising from Valoria. It was an ancient one, given to this region of the world to aid the people in need. One that speaks from the heart to the Creator and surrenders to His will. Once, the song was sung by all, and then slowly, it became quiet and was no longer heard."

Enlin bent over a Knight who still breathed, motioning for Rylan to help him tend to the wound on his stomach that bled heavily. "One of the soldiers has gone for supplies and the Physician," Rylan murmured softly so as not to interrupt Breeon.

"I was lost to the Fallen at the moment my wings separated completely from my body. They change then, into an iridescent glimmer that is unseen. They fell with me. The fight had put me over the Silvanna Woods, and it was there that without my wings, I became as all of you are, the memory of what I had been gone with my lost wings. A separation of my mind to keep my true identity buried deep."

She came to Enlin then, kneeling in front of him to look into his eyes, reaching out to take his face into her hands. "That is how I came to you. Lost, human, with no deception behind my memory loss. I knew things of this world because I have spent time here, but not as a part of it."

Breeon tilted his head with her hand, her fingers examining the wound on his jaw. She tore a strip from the hem of her shift and pressed it against the blood that still seeped from the cut. She was gentle and so close he was able to see the faint hovering of light on her skin, the gold flecks reminding him of dust in a ray of sunlight.

"How much of the blood on you is yours?" Enlin ran his carefully hands down her arms.

"Nothing that requires immediate attention."

"What happens now?" he asked.

Her eyes shifted to the side, and she eased back as the Physician bent beside him with his bag of supplies.

"Your Kingdom will not fall. It has been tested and found worthy. Your heart holds much love for your people and hungers for knowledge of the Creator. If you place your trust and faith in Him, He shall guide you as you restore what He has given you."

Breeon rose, holding his gaze for several long moments. "I will go and see to Nyala and Velynn. They are hiding and frightened."

"Breeon..."

She turned back. "We shall speak again," she assured him, and he was glad she had deciphered his thoughts. With those around offering medical care, there were too many listening ears.

She left him in the care of the Physician and Enlin impatiently endured the ministrations. As before, there was much to be seen to. Bodies to be gathered and buried, families he would have to speak to, briefing with the Council, and Viker still waiting for his indictment.

Enlin wanted to forgo it all in favor of sitting with his wife before the fire to learn more about the events both past and future that had brought them together and seemed to be what would also separate them.

Duty took his attention elsewhere as soon as the Physician declared him well enough and gave him orders to rest.

Garin, sporting many bandages of his own, was waiting for him.

"Report?" Enlin requested.

"Nyala is fine. She was with the Queen and the servant girl.

The Queen assured me there is no more immediate danger, but I have left your sisters in the care of several Valor Knights as a precaution. The Council is being assembled and awaits our presence. Rylan and Weston are passing on orders and will join us shortly."

"How is Alayna?"

"She bears the look Breeon had before... before whatever they did happened, but she is alive. Barely, and I do not know for how long."

Enlin gave Garin a sidelong glance.

"I haven't sorted out my feelings as of yet," Garin responded to the silent question.

"Nya will have to be told."

Garin blew out a long breath. "I have a daughter." He pressed a hand over his heart. "Your Majesty." Garin stopped walking, casting a look about the empty hallway. Most of the men who had fought had been dispersed to other duties. "It may not be wise to change what all believe about Nyala. She has been a Princess all her life. I am not sure I want to take that from her. I understand that is not my choice, but..."

Enlin placed a hand on Garin's shoulder, squeezing. "You are a good man, Garin. You need to take time to consider the consequences of that. She would never know you are her father. We will revisit this conversation another time."

Garin nodded gratefully. "Thank you, Your Majesty."

CHAPTER 32

"Many things that have happened and been said this day cannot be discussed in the presence of the Council," Enlin warned Garin, Rylan and Weston.

"If I may, perhaps your first order of business as King should be to gather a Council you trust implicitly with every detail," Garin suggested. "There is no need to follow the ways of your father if you do not choose to."

Enlin nodded. "Wise words," he acknowledged, looking past the small group of men at his wife as she made her way toward them. He had refused to begin the meeting until she was at his side.

"I shall join you in a moment. I'd like a few minutes alone with the Queen."

No one argued and they entered the room to give him the privacy he wanted. "I have warned them to be careful of the things they share within the room," he told her.

The light that had seemed to hover on her skin had dimmed, giving her the appearance of nothing more than a beautiful woman, rather than the angel she was. "Will you leave, Breeon?" he questioned softly, needing this one answer.

"I need the feather, Enlin."

"I don't know where it is, Breeon. That is the truth."

"We shall speak later. Let us not keep the Council waiting." "The King is dead," Enlin announced, taking control of the meeting immediately. "We believe the Kingdom is no longer in danger, so the coronation will need to commence quickly."

"Your Majesty, I shall see to those details. The loss of the King is a blow but establishing your leadership and authority formally and swiftly will say much on its own." Telphee sported a bruise along the left side of his head and seemed a bit less than his normal focused self. Enlin did not doubt that the King's death was affecting the man. He had served at his side for years.

"Thank you, Telphee. It is good to see you safe."

Telphee nodded.

"I would like to see what we can do to aid King Ardal in his efforts to restore Kingdom Vyell. As our ally, it is important to show our loyalty. Our alliances have proved their worth and I seek to strengthen those relationships in the future."

"An excellent course of action," Garin commended.

"Let us decide how we shall deal with Viker and have that be done." Enlin wanted to find a way to put the short, but devastating war behind them as much as possible.

"Perhaps Telphee could offer you a solution." Breeon spoke and Enlin saw that her eyes were fixed on Telphee, their golden depths cold like the glint of a jewel.

"I... I cannot think why you would think I would have one, Lady Breeon."

"Your Majesty," Enlin corrected with a frown.

"What do you think Viker would say of you if we asked him?" Breeon continued, her words as cold as her eyes.

A flash of anger sparked in Telphee's eyes.

"Breeon?" Enlin said her name quietly, but her hand on his arm stilled him.

"Garin, could you bring Viker?"

Garin stood. "Of course, Your Majesty." He bowed slightly before leaving the room.

Enlin studied Telphee. His shoulders were clenched, his jaw tight, a muscle twitching in his cheek. And his eyes had hardened. Was he upset that he was being challenged or did Breeon have information that would condemn the man? Was it possible she was right?

He thought back over what he knew. The Fallen had been holding Telphee when they had come upon Viker with the King hostage. He had disappeared after. Been missing until his appearance after his sisters had been found. Did it make sense?

Not a word was spoken while they waited. The tension grew. Both in Telphee and the men in the Council. Bodies shifted in chairs; throats were cleared. Telphee maintained his stiff but still posture.

One man jumped when the door opened. Garin and two guards led Viker into the room and guided him to stand at the end of the table, where he could be seen by all.

Viker scanned the table, his eyes stopping to rest on Breeon. He opened his mouth, but she spoke before he could, her words calm but authoritative. "Not one lie shall come from your mouth. You will speak the truth to all assembled, or you will be given over to the Fallen Valley. This is the only grace that shall be offered to you."

Viker licked his dry lips and nodded, his eyes moving to Enlin. "My father was a noble with a thirst to rule. He built an army and took that thirst to conquer small towns, and then cities, and then a small Kingdom your grandfather had culled into his strategy to become an untouchable larger Kingdom."

Running his tongue over his lips again, Viker cleared his throat. His voice was hoarse and one of the Silver Knights near him rose to pour a glass of water, taking it to him and holding it to his lips for him to drink.

"Continue," Enlin ordered when the Knight had sat again.

"That was his mistake. Your grandfather retaliated. It was quick, and it was brutal. Somehow, your former King had befriended the creatures of Shadow Caves and he brought them against my father. I was but a boy, but I was there, watching when your grandfather made his statement with my father's life."

Contempt and hatred filled Viker's eyes. He jerked forward, the guards holding him yanking him back under control. "I vowed to have my revenge," Viker spat out.

He sucked in several long, deep breaths through his nose, glaring at the floor, before he rolled his neck, cracked his jaw, and continued. "Years later, when Telphee approached me with his plan..."

"He lies!" Telphee shouted, bolting up from his chair. The two soldiers that flanked him were just as fast, their hands grabbing his arms, and both pulling their swords to hold them at his throat.

Viker laughed, a short, mirthless sound. "The angel will know if I lie," he tossed at Telphee. His eyes shot to Breeon. "It was a brilliant plan. Telphee had gained the favor of a Fage and told them about a prophecy spoken to the King. A feather from an angel that could give them life."

Baring his teeth around a wicked laugh, he shook against the guard's hold again. "He brought me into his game, gave me the players, and began the strategy. We planned for years before we were handed a golden platter... a missive asking if we knew the identity of a mysterious woman. Telphee, of course, knew of her memory loss and had already spun the scenario to his favor, aligning the woman to you making her the missing piece of our final plan."

He lunged against his captors, toward Telphee, the two closest Knights rising to lend their aid. "If you had not missed details as vital as the sorceress of the woods, we might have claimed our victory!" he shouted angrily.

"Do you think they will stop?" he screamed at Enlin. "They will never stop! They will come for her, again and again! This war will never end!"

"That's enough," Enlin commanded. "Take them both to the dungeons until we decide how to handle their punishments."

It took a few minutes for the room to quiet. "How did you know, Breeon?" Enlin questioned.

"The Fallen leave their mark on all who give themselves over to their wickedness. It clung to Telphee like a fog."

"I am at a loss, Majesty," Rylan exclaimed. "I have served by his side for years! I can't say he was the most pleasant of men to deal with, but I cannot recall ever questioning his loyalty!

What does that reveal about my ability to keep you safe?"

"I was as duped as you," Enlin pointed out.

"What are these Shadow Caves and the creatures that he spoke of?" Elias asked, shooting a questioning glance around at those assembled. "Should we look further into that?"

"The man is half delusional," one of the Councilmen uttered. "Angels and such. There are no such things. His mind was obviously not right."

"I think this has been enough for today," Enlin declared, standing. "I am hungry, and tired, and I would like some time with my wife. Rylan, forgive me for asking, but with Telphee out of the picture, could you take over the details for the coronation?"

"Of course, Your Majesty. I am at your service."

"Thank you. See that a missive is prepared by the Herald to go to Vyell, Garin."

They dispersed, Enlin leading Breeon from the room. He

flagged a servant hovering nearby in case he was needed and requested food be sent to his suite and baths be prepared for both of them. He was sure Breeon was as anxious as he to wash the remnants of battle from her.

Felix and Servin, of the Valor Knight Order, waited outside the doors of Breeon's rooms. They bowed a greeting. "It is clear, Your Majesty. Every crevice has been checked.

Enlin had noticed the glass had been swept from the hallway and the blood mopped up. No bodies had remained. He was grateful and ready for things to return to normal.

"I will see you shortly, Breeon," he promised, and left her for his own room.

CHAPTER 33

*D*ressed in a gown the color of a late sinking sun, Breeon entered his chamber. "There is one thing left to do before we may sit and relax for the evening," she said softly.

"What is it?" Enlin rose from his seat and approached her. "The feather, Enlin. I need it."

Sighing, Enlin nodded. She would not stay with him. The feather was her way back to the place she had come from. "We are fine," he declared to the guards as they left his room. Enlin suspected the feather was in one of the secret places he had not disclosed to the Knights before they had made their way through the hidden passages leading to the King's rooms.

Inside the door, Enlin stopped and looked around. The destruction had been cleared, and the floor was bare of the many rugs that had been spread about. Enlin was sure they had been disposed of, the blood stains making them stark reminders that could not be cleaned.

"I have not yet dealt with the loss of my father. There has. been no time for grief."

Nor was there time now. At the window, Enlin slid his

hand into a crevice and removed the key concealed there. He carried that to a corner of the wall and felt for the tiny holes that would allow him entry into the cavity behind it. From the outside, the thick stone curves of a balcony concealed the width of the small room, and its odd shape was carved out behind a large fireplace in the sitting room beyond.

The key slid into place and turned easily with a soft click. Enlin felt the next column of holes and repeated the process. Twice more and he was able to swing the wall forward to open a narrow entry.

Lighting a candle on one of the tables, Enlin carried it into the room, Breeon behind him. The feather was there, encased in a clear glass rectangular box. It gave off light and looked as though it were suspended in the glass. Gold particles glittered over the delicate shape.

It was magnificent. Enlin turned to Breeon. "What will happen?"

"You have made the choice, Enlin." Breeon lifted the box and left the small area they stood in. Enlin followed her, contemplating her words. He was unsure of their meaning.

He blew out the candle and they left the King's chamber. "Alayna was able to contain what was left of who she was before she chose this world," Breeon said as they walked. "She knew that I was dying. Angels are able to feel things that exist in the supernatural realm, and as the darkness the Fallen brought increased, and the light that gives me life was destroyed, she gathered it deep within her."

"What was destroyed?" Enlin interrupted. "Did my own actions cause you to fall sick?"

"No. When Viker's army and the Fallen were in the Silvanna Woods, they destroyed the feathers of my wings. They are very difficult to see. I am surprised this one was found, but I have been told it was prophesied, so I know our creator meant for it to be here for this moment."

"The feathers are what give you life?" Enlin was doing his best to understand all she was saying.

"The Creator gives me life. The wings are of the heavenly realm. When they are stripped away, we become almost human. The Fallen are those that fell with the Evil one, or those that while on this earth chose to fall prey to sin."

Breeon turned into the suite of rooms reserved for the wounded and sick. There were many soldiers being cared for. "Take us to Alayna, please," Breeon requested of a servant, who bowed and hurried to lead them to a private room.

Enlin shut the door for privacy. Breeon set the glass box on the table beside the bed and touched her fingers to Alayna's heart. Lashes fluttered and a tiny smile was given in response.

"You have given greatly of yourself, Alayna. Now, you must make a choice." Breeon lifted the glass lid from the box and carefully placed the flat bottom where the feather lay upon Alayna's stomach. "I cannot make it for you," Breeon whispered as she stepped back.

"I don't understand," Enlin said. "Why have you brought it to her?"

"I was given my choice when Alayna placed her hands upon me. If I had refused, I would have been taken from this place and gone back to where I came from." She turned her head to meet his eyes. "I... did not want to go."

Before Enlin had a chance to answer, light exploded in the room, blinding him. "Breeon!" His hand found her arm, telling him she still stood beside him. He pulled her close.

It was only seconds before the light faded back into what it had been before. Blinking to clear the spots from his eyes, Enlin saw that Alayna sat up in the bed, the ghostly white of her skin gone. The darkness her hair and eyes had melded to restored.

The blue of her eyes was like the sky again. The color of

her hair like the sun. Enlin smiled when he thought that if his father could see her now, he would be pleased that she was still fitting of the description.

There was no sign of the feather. It had fulfilled its purpose and was gone.

"I will send Garin to you," Breeon said, stepping forward to place a kiss on one of Alayna's rosy cheeks. "I know you both have much to discuss."

Alayna grasped her hand. "Thank you. I know in the days to come, you and I will become friends."

Breeon nodded, and taking Enlin's hand, she was the one who led them from the room.

Once again in the hall outside of the infirmary, alone, she turned to him.

"There was little time to say what needed to be said. I made my choice, even though I was unsure of what you would have chosen."

Enlin lifted his hands to cradle her face. "Breeon. I am enthralled by your strength, your kindness, and already I have made mistakes. But I like you. Perhaps neither of us would have chosen this path, but this Creator you speak of so easily has given you to me, and I intend to do everything in my power to make you happy and be sure that He is pleased with me."

Her lips lifted into a smile. "I am happy to hear you say that Enlin."

Enlin could see no better way to end the conversation than to press his lips to hers, and this time, to make it real.

REVIEW LINK

Did you love Angel Song?
Reviews help authors so much!
Scan the QR code below to go directly to the Review page.
Thank you so much!

WHAT'S NEXT?

The next book in the Kingdom of Silvera is in progress! Stay tuned for updates on any of my social media channels.

Relic, Part II of Mechanical Angel is finished and currently in editing and cover creation.

Plans for 2023 include the next installments in the Chosen Angel Series—the seven trumpets!

ABOUT THE AUTHOR

Sara Shanning tries not to identify with the word 'normal.'

Despite having the same habits as many other writers (coffee addiction) she does her best to put herself into the stories she creates and thus segregate herself from the masses.

As this creation proved, even trying to write a romance that covered all the 'tropes' ended up being near impossible. What was meant to be a fa-la-la-la-la romance soon became a fantasy world all its own. So much more fun to write, and hopefully, so much more fun to read!

If you liked Angel Song, you will be thrilled to learn that while this book was being written, an entire fantasy world took shape in Sara's head and she has plans for more books set within the boundaries of this Kingdom.

READER CHALLENGE:

Tag me on Instagram with a picture of an angel! A book cover, something from Pinterest, a trinket in your home… be creative!

ALSO BY SARA SHANNING

Mechanical Angel

THE CHOSEN ANGEL SERIES

Seal One: Rise of the Antichrist

Seal Two: Dark of War

Seal Three: Starve the Soul

Seal Four: Shadow of Death

Seal Five: Fall of Religion

Seal Six: Rending of the Earth

Seal Seven: Silence of The End

THE AVAH RIVERS BIOGRAPHIES

The Octobers

The Shadows that Hide Me

The Screaming of the Others